Love,
IRL

Kansas City, MO Public Library
00001880027908

Love, IRL

TRACY GOLDFARB

JAMES LORIMER & COMPANY LTD., PUBLISHERS
TORONTO

Copyright © 2020 by Tracy Goldfarb
Published in the United States in 2021.

All rights reserved. No part of this book may be reproduced or transmitted in
any form or by any means, electronic or mechanical, including photocopying,
or by any information storage or retrieval system, without permission in
writing from the publisher.

James Lorimer & Company Ltd., Publishers acknowledges funding support
from the Ontario Arts Council (OAC), an agency of the Government
of Ontario. We acknowledge the support of the Canada Council for the
Arts, which last year invested $153 million to bring the arts to Canadians
throughout the country. This project has been made possible in part by the
Government of Canada and with the support of Ontario Creates.

Cover design: Tyler Cleroux
Cover image: Shutterstock

9781459415652
eBook also available 9781459415638
Cataloguing data for the hardcover edition is available from Library and
Archives Canada.

Library and Archives Canada Cataloguing in Publication (Paperback)

Title: Love, IRL / Tracy Goldfarb.
Other titles: Love, in real life
Names: Goldfarb, Tracy, author.
Series: RealLove.
Description: Series statement: Real love
Identifiers: Canadiana (print) 20200231731 | Canadiana (ebook) 2020023174X
| ISBN 9781459415621 (softcover) | ISBN 9781459415638 (EPUB)
Classification: LCC PS8613.O442 L68 2020 | DDC jC813/.6—dc23

Published by: Distributed in Canada by: Distributed in the US by:
James Lorimer &   Formac Lorimer Books   Lerner Publisher Services
Company Ltd., Publishers   5502 Atlantic Street   1251 Washington Ave. N.
117 Peter Street, Suite 304   Halifax, NS, Canada   Minneapolis, MN, USA
Toronto, ON, Canada   B3H 1G4   55401
M5V 0M3   www.lernerbooks.com
www.lorimer.ca

Printed and bound in Canada.
Manufactured by Marquis in Toronto, Ontario in August 2020.
Job #355205

This book is dedicated to all those teenagers, past and present, who had to turn to a screen to find a home for themselves.

01 *Perfect Match*

Saturday, September 1, 8:26 PM

You've been connected with a stranger. Say hello!

Stranger: hi

You: Hello!

Stranger: pics?

You: Really? That's the first thing you ask?

Stranger: isn't that what people do here?

You: Not if they want to have a real conversation . . .

Stranger: who actually wants a real convo on this site?

You: I do. Why, you don't? Why are you here?

Stranger: if I said sexting would you judge me?

You: Yes.

Stranger: well then . . . I'm here to talk to random people

You: Nice catch.

Stranger: I thought so

so why are you here?

You: I dunno. I'm just bored, I guess? I like talking to strangers online. It doesn't matter what I tell them, we'll never meet again. Y'know?

Stranger: yeah I get that

so is there anything in particular that you want to talk about?

You: Oh, I don't know.

What kind of things do you like?

Stranger: I like reading I guess . . .

You: What do you like to read?

Stranger: well . . .

have you heard of the timetale series?

it's about these kids at a magic school

You: Oh my god, that's my favourite! I love the Timetale Series!

Stranger: books or movies?

You: The books, obviously. Don't get me wrong, the movies are fine. But the books are SO much better. They go into more detail, you actually get to learn about the characters and what makes them tick.

Stranger: and I thought I was a dork

You: Haha, sorry. I get a little nerdy when I'm talking about things I like.

Stranger: don't be sorry

tts is my favourite

You: Who's your favourite character?

Stranger: seith

You: Oh my god, SAME! I love the way they've developed his arc. And the fact that they weren't afraid to make an openly gay character!

Stranger: I think the main guy is still gonna end up with a girl though that's how books like this work

You: I dunno, I have faith that the author will be willing to change things up a bit . . . Imagine a queer couple as the main love interest!

Stranger: it's not gonna happen

when book seven comes out I'll get to say I told you so

You: How? We're on RandoChat. It'd be impossible to match with me again . . .

Stranger: you could always give me your email address

that is

if you wanted to continue talking

You: . . .

that was pretty smooth :P

Maybe at the end of the chat . . .

Stranger: cool

You: So . . .

What do you do? Are you in school?

Stranger: I'm in high school

what about you mr timetale

what do you study?

You: How do you know I'm a guy?

Stranger: just a hunch

You: Well, I am, but you shouldn't assume that.

Stranger: but I was right

You: And how do you know I'm in school?

Stranger: another educated guess

You: Do elaborate, please. How did you make an "educated guess" about my age?

Stranger: well you like tts

if you were that much older than me you probably wouldn't have
read the books

if you were that much younger than me you wouldn't have grown
up with the books and would probably like the movies more

so I'm guessing you're 17–18ish

I bet I can even guess where you live

You: How?

Stranger: well

you added a u to favourite so you're not american

I'm gonna guess you're in canada like me

because if you were in australia or uk or something it would be
pretty late

tell me if I'm way off base

You: . . .

Stranger: yeah that's what I thought

so mr teenager in canada

what can I call you?

other than stranger, of course

You: . . .

You first.

Actually . . .

Can we use nicknames? Is that okay? I just . . .

It's weird giving out my name to someone on the internet, y'know?

Stranger: sure

I'm . . . dorian

19

I live in ontario

your turn

You: I'm Tristan. 17, turning 18. Also Ontario. Please don't stalk me.

Stranger: I promise I won't

anyway you have as much information on me now as I have on you

You: So the name Dorian . . . where'd that come from?

Stranger: based on a book I used to like in middle school

thought it was cool at the time and it just kinda stuck

my email address is even dorian_green@gouglemail.com

how'd you get the name tristan?

You: It's from Arthurian legend. He's one of the knights of the round table.

Okay, enough about my nerdiness. Let's talk about something less humiliating!

Stranger: lol okay

You: Oh, shoot . . . I just noticed the time. I've gotta run.

Stranger: oh

it was really awesome talking to you

honestly

if you wanna keep chatting later you can always give me your email address

or add me to instachat

but only if you want

You: Oh! Yeah! I forgot that! I'm tristan-ofthe-roundtable@ gouglemail.com

It was awesome talking to you, too! I hope we can do it again sometime.

Stranger: yeah same

You: Bye!

Stranger: bye

You have disconnected from the chat. To start another chat with a stranger, click here.

02 Stuck in Class

Wednesday, September 5, 8:45 AM

Alex surveyed the classroom and chewed his lip in contemplation. He had thought the class would be full. But it was already 8:45 and there were only ten other students in the room, scattered around on uncomfortable chairs and their too-small desks.

Alex grumbled as he squirmed in his seat, trying to write with his left hand on the offensively right-handed table. His mind wandered briefly to the conversation he'd had on RandoChat the previous night and debated whether he wanted to contact Dorian when he got home.

As the teacher droned on, Alex picked up his pen. He chewed the end of it and glanced around the room, taking in his classmates.

On one side of the room was Man-Bun. He and his friend were talking in hushed voices. Man-Bun's friend didn't notice when the teacher glared at her before continuing his introduction.

On Alex's right was Ponytail. She had glasses and was furiously writing notes in a little pink book, her pen scratching back and forth across the page.

Sitting at the back of the classroom, far from the teacher, was Too Cool for School. His feet were up on the desk and his arms crossed over his chest. He was probably asleep behind his sunglasses. He had long, dark hair tied back in a ponytail, and a smirk lingering on his lips.

". . . Now then, I am Mr. Hammond. Welcome to my class."

Mr. Hammond looked to be in his mid-thirties, with short, greying hair and laugh lines beginning to crease around his eyes. He had a pair of glasses that he would sometimes take off and wave around while making a point. Then he would notice them in his hand and place them back on his face. He sat on the edge of his desk and made pop culture references that Alex didn't understand, before joking about dating himself.

As the class went on, Alex found he enjoyed listening to Hammond and his introduction. English had never been Alex's favourite subject, but the teacher made it slightly more interesting than he had expected. One thing Alex did not enjoy, however, was the rest of the class. Man-Bun asked obvious questions about things that Alex considered common knowledge. Ponytail's hand would shoot up as soon as Hammond asked the students anything.

The worst classmate of all was Too Cool for School. The guy argued about everything, which Alex found immensely annoying. It also got the lesson off track, and Alex was hoping this first class would end early.

"Just shut *up*," Alex muttered under his breath the third time Too Cool for School interrupted the class.

"Sir, I realize Shakespeare is commonly taught in English courses," Too Cool for School was saying. "But don't you think it would be better to discuss a writer who's less . . . *dead?*"

Alex let out a groan as he leaned back in his chair. Too Cool for School was good looking, but not *nearly* enough to make up for his attitude.

"Would you ask me to teach a music course without covering Bach and Mozart?" Hammond responded with a grin. "Does Beethoven not get an honourable mention?"

Don't encourage him, Alex thought. He hated that the teacher validated Too Cool, playing along with his ridiculous questions.

"If it was a course in Rock and Roll, then yeah, probably," said Too Cool.

"Ah, yes. I understand your confusion." Mr. Hammond smirked and removed his glasses. "This course is meant to introduce you to the history of literature. Here, you're getting an overview, from early authors to the most recent ones. I'm giving you the *Cole's Notes* version of English writing. Anything else you want to learn, you're welcome to study on your own time."

Too Cool for School crossed his arms again and rocked onto the back legs of his chair. He was apparently satisfied with the teacher's answer.

"Any other questions before I continue?" asked Hammond.

Ponytail's hand shot up. Alex knew, right then and there, that it was going to be a very long term.

03 Dorky in the Best Way

Wednesday, September 5, 5:17 PM

Tristan: Hey stranger!

Dorian: hey

Tristan: What's up?

Dorian: nm, you?

Tristan: You know, you're making it really difficult to have a real conversation.

Dorian: lol sorry

has your school started yet?

Tristan: Yeah, it just started today.

Dorian: same

how was your first day

Tristan: Meh . . .

Dorian: that good eh?

Tristan: Yeah, it wasn't quite what I expected.

Dorian: howso?

Tristan: I don't know. I'm in a new school . . . I just thought everyone here would be like me, you know? There to actually learn. Instead, they're just . . . there.

Dorian: I'm sure some of them are there to learn

Tristan: Not really. I mean, yeah, there seem to be a few students here and there that wanna study and stuff but . . .

Okay, so, my first class this morning, not a single person was listening to the teacher.

Dorian: you were

Tristan: Yeah, I was, but no one else.

I just expected grade 12 to be more . . . intelligent?

Dorian: intelligent?

Tristan: Yeah. Intelligent. A lot of the kids in the class have no idea what they're talking about and it's annoying.

Dorian: did you ever think that's why they're at school?

Tristan: What?

Dorian: they don't know what they're talking about

maybe they're there to learn, yknow?

Tristan: Hey! Whose side are you on, anyway?

Dorian: I'm sorry

please go on about how everyone in your class is an idiot

Tristan: I never said that.

Dorian: you were thinking it

Tristan: Ugggh. I just . . .

So there's this guy in my class who keeps trying to argue with the teacher and I just . . . I just want to yell at him to shut up and let the class happen!

Dorian: some people like to argue

I do

Tristan: I can see that!

Dorian: ouch

my poor ego

it hurts

Tristan: Oh, shut up. :P

Dorian: I can never go on

the pain

Tristan: I don't get why they won't just listen to the teacher.

Dorian: calm down tris

Tristan: Anyway . . .

How was your first day? Do you like your classes?

Dorian: they're fine

I took a year off last year

so it's kind of weird to be back

and it's only the first day of class

not like you learn anything on the first day

Tristan: I suppose not.

Dorian: ask me in a few weeks I'll probably know by then

Tristan: Will do. We just have to hope you haven't stopped talking

to me by then!

Dorian: why would I stop talking to you?

Tristan: Because I'm a dork? I don't know . . .

It was a joke!

Dorian: but I enjoy talking to you

Tristan: Well, thanks. :)

Dorian: don't get cocky

you're just the only dude I know who'll actually talk about tts with me might as well keep you around a bit longer

Tristan: And he's back.

Dorian: ?

Tristan: The Dorian we all know and love.

Dorian: oh yeah

the one who's a complete dick

Tristan: That's the one!

Dorian: lol

hey random question . . .

do you watch basker?

it's that new cartoon about this kid and his quest to discover magic

Tristan: Yes! I love that show!

Dorian: did you see the latest episode?

Tristan: Oh my god, I've had nobody to talk to about it!

It was awesome, wasn't it?!

When they killed his brother, I was all like "WHAT?!?" Could NOT

believe they did that!!

Dorian: lol

you're such a dork

Tristan: Hey!

Dorian: I mean it in the best way

Tristan: Haha . . . Okay, fine.

Dorian: so what're you up to now

Tristan: Making dinner. Apparently I have to do that these days.

Dorian: these days?

Tristan: Mom's been super busy so I have to actually feed myself. :P

Dorian: oh

what's for dinner

Tristan: Pasta. It's easy. The sauce comes in a can. You can't really go wrong with it. And I'll have lunch for tomorrow, too. Hooray, leftovers!

Dorian: lol

Tristan: Okay, I'll be back. Gonna go eat.

Dorian: actually, I g2g

sorry

Tristan: Oh! Okay.

I guess I'll talk to you tomorrow?

Dorian?

Okay . . . Well, bye!

Thursday, September 6, 6:11 PM

Tristan: Hey, what happened to you last night?

Dorian: hey sorry about that

roommate needed me for something

Tristan: That's fine! Just glad you're okay!

I didn't realize you had a roommate. You don't live with your parents?

Dorian: nah

live with my friend

he took me in when I ran away from home

he used to go to my school but he graduated last year so we

share a place near his university

Tristan: What?!

Dorian: yeah, he's been great

Tristan: You . . . ran away from home?

Dorian: oh yeah

Tristan: I'm so sorry to hear that.

I didn't realize.

Dorian: it's fine

it happened a while ago

Tristan: I'm sorry.

Dorian: don't apologize

you didn't make me leave

Tristan: May I ask what happened?

Dorian: oh the usual crap

shitty family shitty life

went to my best friend's place and now we're roommates

Tristan: I'm sorry . . .

Dorian: don't be

it's the past

tris?

you still there?

Tristan: Yeah.

Dorian: how were classes today?

Tristan: Fine.

Dorian: no insufferable classmates this time?

Tristan: Eh . . .

Dorian: tristan I'm fine

don't worry about me

Tristan: What? I wasn't worried.

Dorian: one word answers are my thing not yours

look I'm not mad at you or anything

Tristan: I know.

Dorian: then stop being so . . .

whatever it is you're being

and start talking in full sentences again

Tristan: I'm sorry.

Dorian: you apologize a lot you know that?

we're gonna have to give you like a swear jar or something

but for sorrys

a sorry jar

every time you apologize you put a dollar in

Tristan: Yeah, I'd be broke by Christmas.

Dorian: earlier even

how about a dime?

Tristan: You're not serious, are you?

Dorian: lol yeah I am

every time you apologize you put a dime in the jar

Tristan: Yeah? And what do I do with all those coins when I'm done?

Dorian: you could send them to me

Tristan: You wish.

Dorian: save them until the jar gets full

use the money to come visit me

Tristan: Oh yeah. Gonna drive to who knows where to go visit an internet stranger with money that he made me save up from apologies. That's safe.

Dorian: we'll figure out what to do with the money later

do you have your jar?

Tristan: No! I'm not doing that!

Dorian: get a jar tristan

go get a jar

I'm gonna stop talking to you until you get a jar

Tristan: FINE. I have a jar. Happy now?

Dorian: I'm never happy

Tristan: Poor Dorian.

Dorian: shit . . . it's almost midnight

Tristan: Oh, wow. It's easy to lose track of time when we talk.

Maybe we should talk less. :P

Dorian: you wound me tris

Tristan: Aw, come on. You know I was kidding.

Dorian: nope

damage was done

I'll never be the same

Tristan: Goodnight, Dorian.

Dorian: woe is me

night

04 *Friends*

Friday, September 7, 6:32 PM

Dorian: what up?

Tristan: Hey.

Dorian: how was your first week?

Tristan: Eh . . . not quite how I wanted grade 12 to be.

Dorian: still mad about the idiots in your class?

Tristan: Not to sound conceited or anything . . .

We're learning some pretty basic stuff . . .

Dorian: you do

Tristan: I do what?

Dorian: sound conceited

Tristan: Ouch.

Dorian: just remember that even if they don't know everything

you know it doesn't make them stupid

everyone's there to learn tris

Tristan: Thanks for calling me out . . .

Dorian: I bring the hard truths

hey I don't judge you

I used to be a lot like that

took spending time with aj to realize that smart comes in all

shapes and sizes

Tristan: AJ?

Dorian: yeah he's my roommate

I used to think he was kind of an idiot

took seeing him in his element to realize that him not knowing

stuff didn't make him stupid

y'know?

Tristan: I guess . . .

Dorian: look just don't judge people based on what they seem like

they can surprise you

Tristan: I suppose so.

Dorian: hey you watching basker on monday?

Tristan: Of course!

Dorian: wanna watch it with me?

Tristan: How would we do that?

Dorian: well

we both watch it and we're both on the computer and we can

talk about it and stuff

nevermind it's a dumb idea

Tristan: No! No, it's a good idea! A great one!

Yeah, I'd love to watch it with you!

Dorian: you sure?

Tristan: Yes. I'm sure. It'll be awesome.

Dorian: cool

Tristan: So how was your day?

Have you decided if you like your classes yet? Or do you need the

rest of the year?

Dorian: I don't need the whole year

gimme maybe six months

Tristan: Hahaha

Okay, remind me to come back to this in six months.

Dorian: will do

yeah school's fine

oh shit

I completely forgot

I g2g

tonight's boardgame night with some friends

Tristan: Oh, okay.

Have fun!

Dorian: thanks

I'll try

but it won't be as much fun as talking to you

Tristan: Haha.

Dorian: I'm not kidding

Tristan: Oh . . . um . . . thanks?

Dorian: bye

Tristan: Bye!

Saturday, September 8, 11:24 AM

Dorian: morning

Tristan: Good morning!

Dorian: any plans for this lovely saturday?

Tristan: I think you need friends in order to have plans.

Dorian: nah

you can have plans by yourself

and what am I chopped liver?

Tristan: We've known each other for a week.

Dorian: so you don't think of me as a friend?

Tristan: It's not that . . . It's just . . .

We haven't really known each other for a long time.

Dorian: I'm wounded

gravely insulted

Tristan: You're my friend!

We're friends! I'm sorry!

Dorian: ten cents

Tristan: What?

Dorian: ten cents

Tristan: What are you talking about?

Dorian: put a dime in the jar

you apologized

Tristan: I had a good reason to apologize!

Dorian: no you didn't

Tristan: I did! I hurt your feelings, so I apologized!

Dorian: you knew I was joking

now put a dime in the jar

Tristan: FINE.

Dorian: you've got to actually do it

Tristan: I WILL.

Dorian: promise?

Tristan: YES.

Dorian: good

Tristan: I do see you as a friend, though.

Dorian: i know

dw about it

Tristan: Okay.

So, what are your plans for today?

Dorian: aj has a date and I'm crashing it

Tristan: Really?

Dorian: nah

he's taking her to the coffee shop that I work at

Tristan: You work in a coffee shop?

Dorian: yeah

it was the only job I could get that would work around school

Tristan: That must suck.

Dorian: it does

but a job's a job

yknow?

Tristan: Yeah . . .

Dorian: k I g2g to work

see you in a bit

Tristan: See ya!

6:42 PM

Dorian: hey

Tristan: Welcome back. How was your shift?

Dorian: it sucked

Tristan: :(

Dorian: meh nbd

Tristan: How was your friend's date?

Dorian: she's way out of his league

Tristan: That's not very nice.

Dorian: lol

doesn't make it any less true

anyways

I don't think she's gonna go on a second date with him

Tristan: That's too bad.

Dorian: if I have to hear one more speech about her stupid brown fawn eyes I think I might kill him

Tristan: Ahahaha!

Remind me to never tell you about my crushes!

Dorian: does that mean you have a crush?

Tristan: Wouldn't you like to know!

Dorian: lol

alright

I'm off

see you tomorrow

Tristan: G'night!

Dorian: night

05 Love in the Air

Sunday, September 9, 7:52 PM

Dorian: hey

Tristan: Hey!

Dorian: how was your day?

Tristan: It's better now.

Dorian: lol

so . . . you excited to watch tomorrow's episode of basker with me?

Tristan: Yes!

I can't wait!

Dorian: cool

I like the idea of watching stuff with you tris

Tristan: Same.

Dorian: shit

aj is home

Tristan: Oh, do you have to go?

Dorian: nah

I don't think so

he just came back from a date though

Tristan: Thought you said she wouldn't go on a second date with him?

Dorian: that's what I thought

guess I was wrong

damn

he brought her home

Tristan: What's wrong with him bringing a girl home?

Dorian: I really don't want to have to meet little miss bambi with her big brown eyes

but he's gonna make me meet her anyway

Tristan: I mean, it can't be that bad . . .

He's your best friend, and he likes her. Maybe you should try to get to know her?

Dorian: easier said than done

god dammit

I have to go

ttyl

Tristan: Bye!

Have fun meeting Bambi!

Monday, September 10, 9:59 PM

Tristan: Hey!

Dorian: whats up tris

Tristan: Not much. Second week of school, same old . . . you?

Dorian: I had work all evening

Tristan: How was work?

Dorian: crappy

Tristan: That sucks . . . I'm sorry.

Dorian: ten cents

Tristan: That was an empathetic sorry! It wasn't an apology!!

Dorian: ten cents

put it in the jar

Tristan: 😊

Dorian: ready for tonight's episode?

Tristan: Yeah!

Wait, don't change the subject!

Why was work so awful?

Dorian: aj and his chick

Tristan: Oh? Your roommate is still with the girl who "wouldn't give him a second date"?

Dorian: they're inseparable

it's awful

Tristan: How was hanging out with her last night?

Dorian: garbage

Tristan: Why? Is she really that bad?

Dorian: she's not bad

it's just he just won't shut up about her

bambi this bambi that

oh her hair is so pretty

oh her freckles are so cute

Tristan: Have you told your friend how you feel?

Dorian: what? no

Tristan: Why not?

Dorian: cause he'd hate me

Tristan: You should tell him.

He's your best friend. Shouldn't you at least try to talk to him and explain what's going on?

Dorian: shut up

Tristan: It hurts because it's true.

Dorian: how's your problem with your dumb classmates?

Tristan: Way to steer the conversation. Very subtle.

Dorian: it's an art

Tristan: I think you should talk to AJ. Be honest with him.

Dorian: tristan . . .

Tristan: All right, all right! Consider it dropped!

What do you think is gonna happen tonight?

Dorian: flashback episode

Tristan: Why do you think that?

Dorian: shows like this always have a good flashback episode after a major character death

Tristan: Huh . . . I never thought about that before.

Dorian: I mean I could be wrong

Tristan: We'll just have to see then, won't we!

Oh my god, you called it! It's a flashback!

How did you guess that?!

Dorian: I dunno

intuition?

Tristan: You must be some kind of genius!

Dorian: nah

I just notice stuff sometimes

that's kinda my thing

Tristan: Well, you're really good at it.

Dorian: lol thanks

Tristan: Hey, I have to go soon. I'm sorry.

Dorian: ten cents

Tristan: What? No! That doesn't count!

Dorian: unnecessary apology

ten cents

Tristan: I hate you.

Dorian: I know

where you off to tonight?

Tristan: I have a friend coming over.

Dorian: thought you said you didn't have any friends

Tristan: I mean, I don't have a lot of friends . . .

I don't really get to see this friend that often. She graduated last year, so we're catching up.

Dorian: sounds fun

tell her I said hi

Tristan: Oh yeah. I'll let her know that the stranger I've been talking to on the internet says hi.

Dorian: lol

cya

Tristan: Bye!

Tuesday, September 11, 5:31 PM

Tristan: Hey!

Dorian: hey

Tristan: How're you?

Dorian: fine

Tristan: What's wrong?

Dorian: what? nothing

Tristan: Oh, you just seemed a little off or something . . .

Dorian: I'm fine

just pissed

aj and his bambi

Tristan: Oh yeah . . .

How's that going?

Dorian: they just started dating

why does she always have to be over at our place?

Tristan: Oh, come on. They're young and in love.

Dorian: screw love

Tristan: You're such a romantic.

Dorian: it's part of my charm

Tristan: Love must be in the air these days. My friend from last night just started dating someone. It was our first time seeing each other in a while and all she could talk about was this dude.

Dorian: gross

Tristan: I mean, it sucked that she didn't really want to talk about anything else. But I'm happy for her, you know? It's nice seeing her like this.

Are any of these life lessons useful to you?

Dorian: screw you

Tristan: Anyway . . .

What're you up to?

Dorian: nothing really

wanna watch something?

Tristan: Sure! Any ideas of what you want to watch?

Dorian: nope

any suggestions?

Tristan: Well, there's that one show by the same guys who made

Basker . . .

Dorian: cool

let's watch that

Tristan: Right now?

Dorian: yeah

Tristan: Okay, let's do it!

Dorian: hang on

lemme find it on metube

ok got it

ready?

Tristan: Yup! Play!

Dorian: playing

Tristan: It wasn't as good as Basker, but it was all right, I guess.

Dorian: ya I'd watch another episode

Tristan: Man, I wish I could watch more. But tomorrow's an early day. Gonna head to bed now.

Dorian: have fun in class tomorrow

Tristan: Thanks, you too!

See you!

Dorian: bye

06 One Chance

Wednesday, September 12, 8:45 AM

Alex sat in his usual seat, anxiously waiting. It was already a quarter to nine, and the class still hadn't started. Alex's leg bounced, and he tapped his pen against the tiny desk attached to his chair.

"All right, class," Mr. Hammond began. "Today you receive your first assignment. I've sorted you into pairs. Together, you will create a Shakespearean dialogue, keeping with his themes and writing style."

Alex smiled to himself. He had done the required reading, so this assignment would be easy.

"I hope everyone here did last week's readings," Hammond echoed Alex's thoughts. "You can get started on your assignment today. It's due in two weeks. The assignment sheet is being passed around. Make sure you take one. When I call your name, please put your hand up so that you can easily find your partner."

Alex ignored the first few names that the teacher called out. He was focused on the ideas bubbling up in his head.

". . . Alejandro Marquez?"

Alex's hand shot up. "It's Alex," he said as he raised his head and searched the room for whoever would end up being his partner.

"You're partnered with Jacob Greenspan."

In the back of the room, Too Cool for School slowly raised his hand. A smirk tugged at the corner of his lips. Alex stared in disbelief before looking back at the teacher and silently pleading that it was some kind of mistake. Ponytail he could have handled. She seemed like she'd at least take the project seriously. Even Man-Bun would have been okay — he probably would have just let Alex take control of the assignment. But Too Cool for School? As attractive as he was, Alex already found him too annoying to want to work with him.

Alex closed his eyes and took a deep breath. He remembered the advice Dorian had given him: *don't judge people on how they seem.*

You get one chance, Mr. Greenspan, Alex thought.

When Mr. Hammond finished assigning the pairings, the students stood up and rearranged themselves. Jacob remained seated. *I guess he expects me to go to him,* Alex thought. With a groan, Alex gathered his stuff and trudged towards the back of the room.

He settled into the chair next to his partner. "Hi, Jacob," he muttered as he pulled his pen and notebook from his bag.

"Hey," Jacob responded. "Call me Jake." The sunglasses stayed on.

Alex had no idea what direction this boy was looking in and he found it unnerving. He opened his notebook and flipped through the pages until he got to his notes on Shakespeare. He was just about to speak when Jake cut him off.

"So I was thinking we should use characters from modern popular culture. And we should go out on a limb and write it in iambic pentameter or something."

Alex suppressed a groan and willed himself not to roll his eyes. All of Alex's ideas had been simple, textbook — ideas that would earn him a decent mark. Jake was making things as complicated as possible.

"Maybe we should go with something a bit . . . simpler?" Alex's voice was so soft, he could barely hear himself over the murmur of the class.

Jake sighed and leaned forward in his chair, bringing himself closer to Alex. He took off his sunglasses, revealing piercing grey eyes that bored into Alex as they searched for something.

"Look," said Jake. "We'll have more fun with the assignment if we do something challenging. Something the teacher hasn't seen before."

Alex clenched his teeth. He needed to keep his

cool around his partner. "I think we should stick with something we know."

"That's the point of Shakespeare! To take what's already established and turn it on its head! That was his whole thing!" Jake's arms gestured wildly in the air.

No, the point of Shakespeare is to get a good enough mark to boost my average, thought Alex.

But he realized that Jacob Greenspan didn't care about marks. With a resigned sigh, Alex leaned back in his chair and closed his eyes, trying to gather his thoughts.

"Fine," he muttered at last. It was much easier to agree with Jake's terrible plan than it was to argue with him. "Whatever you want."

"Right . . ." Jake raised an eyebrow at Alex before shrugging. "Okay, then, here's what I was thinking . . ."

English was quickly becoming Alex's least favourite subject.

07 *Good Advice*

Wednesday, September 12, 5:26 PM

Dorian: hey

Tristan: Hey.

Dorian: how was class today?

Tristan: Garbage.

Dorian: what happened?

Tristan: Nah, you don't want to hear me complain . . .

Dorian: I wouldn't ask if I didn't want to hear it

Tristan: You sure?

Dorian: yup

Tristan: Okay . . .

So we have this assignment, right? And I got paired with the one guy in class who doesn't care about getting good grades! He's so frustrating. I have no idea how to work with him. It's just . . . jshdhsjsks

Dorian: wow

you really are mad

Tristan: SO angry! Why does this always happen?! I don't need some guy who doesn't give a damn about his marks to ruin things for me!

aldjdhdhfjfka

!!!!!!!

Dorian: you want advice or do you just need me to listen?

Tristan: I dunno . . . whatever you want.

Dorian: advice it is

give him a chance

I know it sounds like crappy advice

but he might end up surprising you

tris?

Tristan: Yeah, I'm still here . . .

Dorian: you gonna respond?

Tristan: I don't know . . .

I just don't know how to respond . . .

I mean, I guess you're right.

But he's always dicking around. He doesn't take anything seriously!

Dorian: have you ever stopped to think maybe you take things too seriously?

Tristan: Shut up.

Dorian: I honestly think you should loosen up and be less . . .

uptight

it might do your blood pressure some good

Tristan: So how were your classes?

Dorian: not bad

we're also doing a group assignment

my partner seems fine

doesn't talk much

I'm thinking I might end up having to do the project on my own

but whatever

I know what I'm doing

and I don't really care if he gets a good grade because of me

I'm not really at school for marks

I'm here to learn

Tristan: I wish I could be that carefree . . .

Dorian: yeah you should try it some time

Tristan: Oh, yeah, you're one to talk. How's your Bambi problem?

Dorian: totally different issue

anyways

we were pointing out your flaws not mine

Tristan: Ha.

Dorian: and to answer your question

not great

aj invited her to boardgame night

that was our thing

just the three of us

spud aj and I

and now he's invited this chick I don't even know

Tristan: I'm sorry . . .

Dorian: ten cents

Tristan: IT WAS AN EMPATHETIC APOLOGY!!

Dorian: and it just cost you ten cents

Tristan: Okay, well, I was gonna give you advice, but now you don't deserve it.

Seriously, though . . .

I get your desire to keep things the same . . .

But sometimes change is good, you know?

Take my friend for example . . . Let's call her Rose.

She spent so long with this guy she was comfortable with, because he loved her. But she never really felt the same way. She finally dumped him. And now she's seeing a new guy that makes her so happy. I haven't seen Rose smile that much in a long time.

I just . . .

I think change can be a good thing.

Dorian?

Dorian: yeah yeah

I'm still here

just mulling stuff over

Tristan: Mull out loud?

Dorian: ok

I'm happy for your friend

but it's not the same as my situation

she left some turd for a better dude

are you saying I'm the turd in this scenario?

Tristan: No! That's not at all what I'm saying!

You're the Rose here!

Things aren't where you want them to be in one relationship. So maybe some change is good?

Dorian: it's not the same tris

I appreciate you trying but these are two completely different things

aj and I are tight

but now bambi's here and she's all he can talk about

I'm not leaving aj because I want to

aj is leaving me . . .

for her

Tristan: Okay, listen up, Dorian. AJ is not LEAVING you! You're making it sound like you two are dating! You're not, are you?

Dorian: no of course not

he's my best friend

Tristan: Exactly! AJ and you will always be best friends, with or without Bambi.

Have you talked to AJ about any of this?

Dorian: no

Tristan: You should.

Dorian: it won't end well

Tristan: Please?

For me?

I would feel better knowing that you spoke to your friend and sorted this out.

Dorian: fine I'll talk to him

you're an annoying little shit you know that?

Tristan: Yeah, but you love it.

Dorian: hey wanna watch another episode of that other show?

Tristan: Uh, sure, yeah.

It's getting late, though . . .

But I guess I can stay up! It's way more fun hanging with you than going to bed.

Dorian: lol

crap . . .

aj just got home

he's calling me I g2g

Tristan: That's fine! We can always watch another night!

I'll speak to you tomorrow!

Goodnight, Dorian!

08 *Lucky*

Thursday, September 13, 4:42 PM

Dorian: I hate him

I frikkin hate him!!!

Tristan: Well, hello to you too.

Dorian: sorry

hi

frikkin aj

Tristan: What did he do?

Dorian: he accused me of being jealous!

says I'm just being a dick because I wish I had a girlfriend like her

Tristan: Did you ever stop to think maybe you are jealous?

Dorian: I swear to god tris . . .

Tristan: Hear me out!

Think about it: why do you dislike her? Maybe you're not jealous about her specifically. But do you think you could be jealous that your friend has a girlfriend and you don't?

Dorian: I don't want a goddamn girlfriend Tristan

Tristan: Cool your jets. I was only asking.

Dorian: screw this

I don't want a frikkin girlfriend

ok

we're friends ya?

Tristan: Of course! I'm sorry!

Dorian: can I tell you something?

something I've never told anyone before

not even aj

Tristan: Yeah, absolutely. I'm here for you. Anything you need.

Dorian: I don't want a girlfriend

ever

I . . .

I think I might like dudes . . .

Tristan?

crap crap crap crap crap

I shouldn't have said anything

shit!!

can we pretend I didn't say that?

I shouldn't have put that on you

Tristan: Dorian!

Stop.

There's no need to freak out.

I'm not judging you. I promise. I just . . .

I needed to figure out how to respond.

Dorian: go ahead

call me a freak

or a homo

or whatever it is you want to call me

Tristan: Shut up.

I would never call you any of those things.

I might call you too dramatic. You really are freaking out over nothing.

Look, Dorian. It's okay. It's totally fine that you're gay. I don't like you any less. I promise.

I just . . .

Dorian: you just don't want to speak to me anymore

Tristan: Let me type, dammit!

I just needed to figure out how to say "me too" without sounding weird.

Dorian?

Jesus, Dorian! For Christ's sake, just say something!

Dorian: really?

Tristan: Really what?

Dorian: you're . . . also gay?

Tristan: Yeah, well, sort of . . .

I mean, I've never actually been with a dude before. But I . . . I do like guys. I'm bi. So, yeah.

And you don't judge me for that, do you?

Dorian: no

no of course not

Tristan: See? So why would I judge you?

Dorian: I just

I've never said any of this out loud before

that was my first time ever admitting it

you know?

Tristan: Yeah . . . I get it. I've been there.

Man, I just want to give you a hug or something. You must be having a really hard time with this.

Dorian: my parents once caught me kissing a dude

it got . . . really bad

I had been thinking about telling aj

but realized that I had to keep quiet

Tristan: That's awful. I am SO sorry that happened to you, Dorian.

Dorian: lol ten cents?

Tristan: Dorian, this is serious.

Dorian: I know I know

I just . . .

I can't tell aj

Tristan: Dorian, do you have a crush on AJ?

Dorian: aj?!?

no!

ew

what?!

that's gross

dude he's like a brother to me

Tristan: I just figured that might be why you're so upset about his girlfriend.

Dorian: no

I'm just

it's always been the two of us

and now

well he's found someone else

and I get left behind

and I know it's not his fault

and he has every right to have a girlfriend and to date her and to fall in love

but it just sucks

because I know I'll never be able to have that

Tristan: What? Why?

Dorian: why what?

Tristan: Why won't you ever be able to have that?

Dorian: I'm gay Tristan

faggots like me don't get to fall in love and be happy

Tristan: All right, let's get one thing straight here.

I just admitted to you that I'm also . . . Well, that I also like guys.

So when you say stuff like that? You're also talking about me. When you make fun of gay people? That's making fun of me.

I get that your go-to is to put yourself down. It's mine too. But you need to understand that when you say homophobic stuff like that, you're also hurting me. Making me feel worse about myself.

Dorian?

You still there?

Dorian: I'm sorry

Tristan: It's okay, Dor. It really is.

It's all okay. It's okay to be scared. And it's okay to not know what the future is gonna bring.

And I care about you. A lot.

And you can always talk to me about any of this. I promise.

Dorian: thanks

Tristan: Dorian, you will find love. You're not hopeless. You're not . . . well, you're not any of those terrible things your parents made you believe. You're amazing.

You're so smart. That's one of the things I like most about you. You're so good at figuring stuff out, like what's gonna happen in the next episode and stuff. And you're so kind. You've been such a good friend to me.

And any guy that gets to have you as a partner is lucky.

So just remember that, okay?

Dor?

Dorian: I'm here . . .

thank you tris

Tristan: You're welcome

Hey, it's getting kind of late . . .

Dorian: can you stay a bit longer?

please?

Tristan: Oh . . . yeah, of course.

Gonna hop into bed though. If I stop replying, I've fallen asleep.

Dorian: that's fine

Tristan: Sorry in advance . . .

Dorian: ten cents

Tristan: How many am I up to now?

Dorian: you're the one who's supposed to keep count

Tristan: Ahaha, okay, I'll count in the morning. Think I've made it to a dollar?

Dorian: possibly

wouldn't put it past you

Tristan: Ahaha

Dorian: anything exciting planned for tomorrow

Tristan: Not really.

You?

Dorian: no

hey tris . . .

you up?

you probably fell asleep

night tris

thanks for everything

just . . .

thank you

so much

see you tomorrow

09 *Still Here for You*

Friday, September 14, 5:12 PM

Dorian: hey tris

Tristan: Hey Dorian.

Dorian: surprised you're still talking to me

Tristan: Shut up. Of course I'm still talking to you.

Who else is gonna put up with my nerdy nonsense?

Or watch shows with me?

Gotta keep you around

Dorian: hey

thanks for last night

Tristan: For what?

Dorian: you know . . .

listening to me

being understanding

not getting mad at some of the stuff I said

Tristan: Any time, Dor.

And I really mean that.

You can talk to me whenever you need to.

Dorian: thanks

so . . .

tonight's boardgame night

and I kinda don't want to go

this'll be the first time since we moved to this place that we'll
have a stranger with us

Tristan: It'll be fine, Dorian. I know it's daunting. I get that you're
scared.

Dorian: I'm not scared

Tristan: Okay, nervous. Whatever.

It'll be okay.

And I'll be right here to talk to whenever you need.

You can say you're going to the bathroom or something and come say hi.

Dorian: you're telling me you're gonna spend all night waiting for me in case I want to talk to you?

that's stupid

Tristan: Don't flatter yourself, I'm only here because I have nothing better to do.

Dorian: ok good

for a moment there I thought you were a really great friend

Tristan: Well, then, I'm glad I dispelled that notion.

It'll be fun, Dor. Just try to relax and not get too stressed.

And remember, she's as scared of you as you are of her.

Dorian: I'm not scared

and I doubt that

Tristan: What, you wouldn't be nervous if your boyfriend invited you to hang out with his friends and his roommate hated you?

Dorian: that requires me having a boyfriend

Tristan: And it requires your boyfriend having friends.

You make a fair point.

Dorian: lol

yeah

only a loser without friends would ever date me

Tristan: I was joking!

I'm sorry . . .

Dorian: ten cents

Tristan: You can shove it up your ass.

Dorian: oh damn tris

never heard you swear before

Tristan: Shut up.

Dorian: lol

I've corrupted you

the devilishly handsome fiend has corrupted the sweet innocent

Tristan

Tristan: Hey, who said I was sweet and innocent?!

Dorian: alright

g2g

Tristan: Have fun, Dorian!

Remember, I'll be here if you need me.

8:03 PM

Dorian: red alert!

tris you there?

Tristan: Yeah, what's up?

Dorian: one hour in and I'm ready to kill her

aj just spent the past thirty minutes trying to explain colonists of cortaan to his girlfriend!!

I've never been more frustrated in my life

Tristan: Deep breaths, Dor.

Dorian: I know how to breathe Tristan!!

Tristan: Dorian!

Don't get mad at me, I'm trying to help.

Dorian: fine

Tristan: Take a deep breath and focus. So what? She doesn't know the game? She's going to learn it and you guys are going to play. Cortaan is better with four people, anyway.

Dorian: you play?

Tristan: Yeah, everyone plays Cortaan. Well, everyone except Bambi. But it's fine. It's an easy game to pick up and you guys will be having fun in no time.

Just try to relax.

Dorian: maybe I'll have a beer tonight in your honour lol

Tristan: Ahaha, sounds good.

Now go back out there and enjoy Cortaan!

10:52 PM

Dorian: hey triiiiiiiiisssssss

Tristan: Hey?

Oh god, are you drunk?

Dorian: looooll just a bit

Tristan: I'm sorry . . .

Dorian: TEN CENTS!!!!!!

Tristan: Ahahaha, okay.

Dorian: naaaaaaah its not your fault

we always drink on boardgame night

jus usually not this much!!!!

its cause aj and bambi and they were all smoochy and I was sick

if it so I had a bit morethan usual

Tristan: Oh my god, you're wasted.

Dorian: shhhhh

Tristan: Ahahahaha!

So does this mean I get to interrogate Drunk Dorian?

Dorian: no need to jnterrogate ill always be honest with you tris

Tristan: Ahahaha

Dorian: maaaaaaaan in so horby

Tristan: Wow, okay, talk about too much information.

Dorian: just gotta fins a guy whod actually wanna have sex eith me!

Tristan: Okay, I think it's time for Drunk Dorian to go get some water and go to bed.

Dorian: noooooooooooo

i wanna talk to my triiiiisttaaaaaaaannnn!!!!

Tristan: Tomorrow, Dorian. We'll talk tomorrow. I promise.

Dorian: nut I have wooork tomorrow

Tristan: Then we talk after work, you idiot.

I'm heading to bed now. You should too. Goodnight, Dorian.

Dorian: byyyeeeeeeeeeeeeeee

10 *Falling*

Saturday, September 15, 6:41 PM

Tristan: How's the hangover?

Dorian: uggggggghhh

Tristan: That bad, eh?

Dorian: I'm sorry about last night

Tristan: Ahahaha, don't be! You were hilarious!

Dorian: I was an idiot

remind me to never get that drunk again

Tristan: Deal.

Dorian: lol

I talked a lot about sex there at the end didn't I . . .

Tristan: Ahaha, yeah. Apparently you were quite "horby" last night!

Dorian: crap

I really am an idiot

Tristan: But you're my idiot!

Dorian: lol

Tristan: Hey, Dor . . .

Can I . . . admit something to you?

Something I've never really talked to anyone about before?

Dorian: you can always talk to me about anything

Tristan: Um . . . I've never actually . . . been with anyone before.

Dorian: as in . . .

Tristan: Been with . . . you know . . .

Dorian: you're a virgin?

Tristan: Thanks for putting it delicately.

Dorian: that's nothing to be ashamed of tris

Tristan: I'm 17, I'm bi and so far in the closet I'm practically in Narnia. I don't think . . . I mean, I'll never really get the chance to do anything. Not any time in the foreseeable future.

Dorian: I hate it when you talk about yourself that way

you're smart

and caring

anyone would be lucky to have you

Tristan: I can't think of a single person who would ever want to "have" me.

Dorian: I would

Tristan: Haha.

Dorian: I'm not kidding tris

Tristan: You have no idea what I look like!

Dorian: I don't need to know what you look like to know that I'm falling for you

tris?

tristan are you there?

crap crap crap crap

I totally scared you off

oh god I've ruined everything

our friendship was good and then I had to go and say a stupid thing like that

Tristan: Shut up, Dor.

Dorian: tris?

Tristan: Just . . . let me type for a second, okay?

Dorian: ok

Tristan: I'm worried you only said that because that's what you thought I wanted to hear.

And I don't want you doing that. Don't say things just because you think I want to hear them.

Dorian: tristan when have you ever known me to do that?

I don't say anything I don't mean

Tristan: How . . .

Dorian: how what?

Tristan: How are you falling for me? You barely know me! And you don't know what I look like!

Dorian: I don't give a crap

talking to you makes me happy

being with you makes me happy

Tristan: Congratulations, you've just described friendship.

Dorian: how often do you want to kiss your friends?

Tristan: What?

Dorian: it's not just friendship if you want to wrap your arms around them

Tristan: What are you saying?

Dorian: I already told you

I'm falling for you

now just . . .

either tell me you like me back or you don't

cause this limbo frikkin sucks

Tristan: Yeah . . .

I do.

I do like you . . . a lot.

I think I get what you mean when you say you're "falling" for me.

Dorian: even though you don't know what I look like?

Tristan: I don't think it matters.

Dorian: I wanna kiss you so badly right now

does that make me weird?

Tristan: No . . . I get what you mean.

I kinda wish I was there beside you . . .

Dorian: with my arms around you

Tristan: Your lips pressed against mine.

Dorian: crap

Tristan: What?

Dorian: we should stop

talking about this I mean

we can talk about other stuff

Tristan: What? Why?! I just confessed my feelings for you!

Dorian: I know and I feel the same way

we established that

Tristan: Then why do you want to change the subject?

Dorian: just away from the kissing and the snuggling and stuff

Tristan: . . .

Dorian: it's . . . you know . . . I dunno . . .

Tristan: No, I don't know.

Dorian: it's kinda got me a bit . . .

and I didn't want things to be awkward or anything

it's fine

ignore me

nevermind

Tristan: Dor, are you okay?

Dorian: yeah I'm good

Tristan: Okay . . .

Umm . . .

So . . .

Dorian: dammit I made things weird again

Tristan: No! Things aren't weird. We're fine. Right? We're fine?

Dorian: we're more than fine

I finally told you how much I care about you

and I found out you like me the same way

Tristan: So I can go back to imagining you here beside me?

Dorian: of course

I'd always be there beside you if I could

Tristan: With your arms wrapped around me?

Dorian: squeezing you tight

keeping you safe

Tristan: I'd be worried, though . . .

If we ever did meet for real.

Dorian: what? why?

Tristan: Well, you know . . .

I'm not really . . . experienced.

Dorian: shut up tris

that doesn't matter to me

you know that

Tristan: Have you?

Dorian: have I what?

Tristan: Ever been with a dude?

Dorian: tris . . .

Tristan: Seriously! Have you?

Dorian: we shouldn't talk about this now

Tristan: Why not?

Dorian: because I'm worried you won't like my answer

Tristan: . . .

Well now you have to answer me, cause I'm terrified!

Dorian: yes

I have

Tristan: One?

Or more?

Dorian: at the same time?

Tristan: Dorian . . .

Dorian: I've been with guys in the past tris

I don't think it's a great idea to go into my sexual history right after I told you I have feelings for you.

Tristan: What's it like?

Dorian: what?

Tristan: Being with a guy.

Or being with anyone.

Dorian: umm

it's good

it's nice

tris why are you asking all this?

Tristan: I dunno. I guess I was just thinking about how it would feel for me to be with you . . .

Dorian: yeah can we go back to talking about other things?

Tristan: Why do you keep trying to change the subject? Do you not want to do that with me?

Dorian: what?

no!

literally the opposite

thinking about you like that . . .

tris I'm kinda turned on

and I know you probably don't want to do stuff in the chat or anything

so I kinda need a cold shower

Tristan: Who said I didn't want to do anything in the chat?

Dorian: . . .

what

Tristan: I never said I wasn't up for that.

I mean, I've been sitting on these feelings and I've liked you for a while. And, well, maybe I've wanted to do this for a while, too.

Dorian: jesus christ tris

Tristan: You don't want to?

Dorian: you have no idea

there's nothing I want to do more

hey . . .

I have an idea

do you wanna maybe hop on voice chat?

so we can . . . hear each other?

Tristan: Yeah, I'd like that. That's a good idea, Dor.

You have started a voice chat with Dorian.

Voice chat with Dorian has ended.

Dorian: that was amazing

you're perfect tristan

you know that?

Tristan: I'm really not.

Dorian: shut up

there's nothing you can say that would ever change my mind

ever

you're my tristan

Tristan: :)

Dorian: lol are you falling asleep?

Tristan: ya

Dorian: well then

goodnight tris

X

11 *Lost and Found*

Sunday, September 16, 11:14 AM

Dorian: hey

tris?

tristan you around?

8:21 PM

Dorian: guess not

well

hope you're okay

getting kind of worried

hopefully I'll talk to you tomorrow

Monday, September 17, 3:12 PM

Dorian: hey tris

off to work

talk to you after?

7:58 PM

Dorian: back

you there?

tristan?

are we not watching basker tonight?

9:11 PM

Dorian: guess not

Tuesday, September 18, 5:22 PM

Dorian: dammit

tris

are you ignoring me because of what we did the other night?

I'm sorry

I didn't mean to do anything to ruin our friendship

I'm so sorry if I did

tristan I just wish you'd talk to me

tell me what's going on

I'm really worried about you

please tristan

I'm sorry

Wednesday, September 19, 6:49 PM

Tristan: Hey.

Dorian: jesus frikkin christ tristan!!

I thought I'd never hear from you again

are you okay?!

what happened?!

Tristan: I'm fine, Dorian. Don't worry.

Dorian: oh thank god

tristan I am so sorry

Tristan: Shut up for a second, okay?

You have no reason to be sorry. None.

You didn't do anything wrong, I promise.

Dorian: then why the hell have you been ignoring me for days?!

Tristan: It's me who should be sorry.

I'm sorry for not responding earlier, I was sorting some things out.

And . . .

I'm sorry for what I'm about to say to you.

Dorian: tristan you're scaring the hell out of me

Tristan: Can you just . . . let me type for the next bit? No interruptions?

Dorian: ok

Tristan: We met on the internet.

I really didn't think anything would come of it, so I didn't say anything earlier.

And we talked about stuff we liked and things we did and it just never came up.

And I'm not one to hide this from people, I'm really not. Like, I'm super open about it in my real life, I just . . .

I didn't expect any of this to happen and then it did and then . . .

And then I fell for you. And you said you fell for me. And it was so nice to hear that, that I didn't even stop to think to tell you . . .

And then we . . . well, in the chat . . . talking about sex and stuff . . . And I just . . . I realized that I had to talk to you about this . . . And I just didn't know how . . .

Dorian: are you still there?

I don't want to interrupt but you haven't said anything in a while tristan what do you have to tell me?

Tristan: Um . . .

I know this means that I might lose you, but you deserve to know the truth, before you get too invested in anything.

I'm trans.

Dorian: you're trans?

Tristan: Yes. I'm trans. I used to have a female body and . . . parts. I've been on HRT for a while now and I've had top surgery and plan to get more surgery once I'm through with high school. It's all complicated. I mean . . . This is . . . part of who I am.

Dorian: and that's why you freaked out and ignored me?

Tristan: Yeah.

Dorian: and this is coming from the guy who was advocating for me to talk to aj about what was bothering me?

Tristan: . . .

Dorian: why didn't you just talk to me?

instead of freaking out

Tristan: Honestly? I thought I'd lose you.

Dorian: what because you're trans?

Tristan: Yes?

Dorian: you think you're the only trans person I've ever met?

don't flatter yourself dork

Tristan: Really?

But all those things you said when you came out to me? All the stuff you were worried about?

Dorian: what . . . I can't be emotional and spout the crap my parents drilled into me?

you know I didn't mean any of it

and I said I was sorry

tris

I stand by what I said the other day

you're perfect

you're my tristan

Tristan: Despite me being trans?

Dorian: no

idiot

not despite anything

I'm crazy about you just the way you are

but I swear to god tris

if you go missing in action on me again I'm gonna kill you

cause you scared the shit out of me

Tristan: I'm so sorry, Dorian.

Dorian: I'm not even gonna charge you for that one

I deserved that apology

I can't believe you stopped talking to me over that

you little shit

Tristan: So you still like me?

Dorian: duh

and you still like me even though I'm cis?

Tristan: Ahaha, yeah. I do.

Dorian: good

cause I was scared for a moment

Tristan: Shut up.

Dorian: make me

Tristan: Thanks, Dor.

Dorian: for what?

Tristan: For caring about me. For liking me despite my momentary freak out and lapse in judgement. For wanting to be my friend.

Dorian: who said I wanted to be your friend?

Tristan: . . . You did?

Dorian: oh I'm sorry

I thought I made it clear

I have absolutely no intention of being your friend

I would however like to be your boyfriend

Tristan: . . .

I almost had a damn heart attack, Dorian! Jesus!

Dorian: lol

so?

Tristan: What do you mean "so"?

Dorian: so how bout it?

wanna be my boyfriend?

Tristan: I've never met you in real life before! How are we gonna date? Is that even possible?

Dorian: where there's a will . . .

Tristan: This is crazy. You're crazy!

Dorian: crazy about you

date me tristan

you know you wanna

Tristan: Fine!

I'll "date" you! Not like anything will be different from how it is now!

Dorian: it'll be different in my heart

Tristan: Idiot.

Dorian: it also means I know you won't run away with another guy

Tristan: Oh yes. Because the boys are lined up at my door, waiting to sweep me off my feet.

Dorian: I would be . . .

if I knew where your door was

Tristan: Shut up.

All right, I have to go. I have a bit of catching up to do. I missed my classes today.

Dorian: what?

why'd you miss class?

Tristan: Damn anxiety. I was freaking out, okay?! I knew I'd have to have this conversation!

Dorian: it ended well

it's all good

drink some tea or something and relax

everything's gonna be fine

Tristan: Thanks.

Okay . . . goodnight Dorian.

Dorian: night tris

x

12 *Talk to Him*

Thursday, September 20, 8:08 PM

Dorian: hey tris x

Tristan: Hey.

Dorian: missed you

Tristan: Dorian, can you not be so . . .

Whatever it is you're being?

Dorian: what are you talking about?

Tristan: I dunno. You're being different. It's weird.

Dorian: you're my boyfriend now

I can be all gross and lovey with you can't I?

Tristan: I just . . . I really want things to be the same as they were before.

I really enjoy being able to come here and have you as my friend.

Dorian: ok

I'm sorry

Tristan: Ten cents?

Dorian: no that only applies to you

Tristan: What? Why? That's not fair!

Dorian: I'm not the one with a problem tristan

so

how was class?

Tristan: Eh . . . not great. I mean, my classes were fine, but I'm gonna have trouble catching up on what I missed.

Dorian: oh shit

Tristan: Yeah, and I have to do that group project at some point.

Oh well, hopefully we can get it done and out of the way.

Dorian: good luck

Tristan: Thanks.

Dorian: so . . .

did you ever end up watching basker?

Tristan: No.

I'm sorry.

Dorian: ten cents

Tristan: No! I'm actually sorry. I just . . . I didn't mean to leave you high and dry like that. I know I promised to watch the show with you, and I feel like an ass for not being there.

Dorian: it's ok

I'm not mad

I was worried but I'm not mad

Tristan: I'm sorry

Dorian: ten cents

that was an extra one

Tristan: FINE.

Ass.

Anyway . . .

Did you end up watching it?

Dorian: nope

Tristan: What? Why?!

Dorian: I didn't want to watch it without you

Tristan: . . .

Okay, that was kinda sweet.

Dorian: lol

anyways we have the rest of the evening to do whatever we want

want to catch up on our show before the internet spoils it for us?

Tristan: Yeah, I'd like that.

Gimme a bit, I need to see if I can find it online.

Dorian: ok

lemme know when it's done downloading

Tristan: Will do.

So how did things work out with AJ and Bambi?

Dorian: eh . . .

aj and I had that fight a while back

then we had boardgame night

and I haven't seen him since

Tristan: Wait, what?

Dorian: yeah

he's spent every night at her place I guess

either that or he's really good at avoiding me

Tristan: Dorian, were you all alone these past few days?

When . . . when I wasn't answering you?

Dorian: ya

Tristan: God, I've been an awful friend. I should've been there for you. I'm so sorry.

Dorian: ten cents

you already apologized twice for that one

Tristan: Stop joking around, Dorian.

Dorian: I'm not joking

put a dime in the jar

Tristan: Fine.

But you were worried about me and I wasn't responding. And you DIDN'T talk to your best friend about it?

Dorian: no?

Tristan: Dor . . .

I think you guys need to have an honest chat to work things out.

Dorian: so when's that episode done downloading?

Tristan: Dorian, don't change the subject.

Dorian: tristan

you're my boyfriend

and you're great

but I'm getting really frustrated

you need to drop it before I get pissed off

Tristan: Fine.

Dorian: thank you

so is that episode done or what?

Tristan: It's done.

Dorian: cool

any thoughts about what might happen?

Tristan: Dunno.

Dorian: ok seriously tristan

what the hell?

Tristan: What?

Dorian: don't 'what?' me

you think I can't tell when you're pissed off?

Tristan: I'm fine.

Dorian: don't be like that tris

Tristan: Dorian, let's just watch Basker.

Dorian: no

Tristan: What do you mean, "no"?

Dorian: I mean no

it's my favourite show

I want to watch it with you when we can both enjoy it

not while you're grumpy

we'll watch it tomorrow

Tristan: I'm not grumpy.

Anyway, isn't tomorrow your boardgame night?

Dorian: ya . . .

I doubt it's still happening

don't think aj is gonna show up

Tristan: He will if you TALK TO HIM.

Dorian: I wouldn't put money on it

Tristan: God dammit, Dorian!! You're so stubborn! You're insufferable sometimes, you know that?

Dorian: so I've been told

and yet I'm not the one who confessed my feelings to someone and then refused to talk to them for three days

Tristan: I said I was sorry! I feel AWFUL about that! You said you weren't mad at me!

Dorian: I'm not

I mean

I'm not thrilled at the whole situation

this past week has really sucked

but I get why you did what you did and I can't be mad at you for that

I just don't like when you bug me about talking to aj

it's hypocritical

I'd have been way more inclined to do that if you had taken your own advice

but it's clearly bad advice

tristan?

Tristan: I'm tired. I'm going to bed.

Dorian: really?

just like that?

you call me insufferable and then you get pissy and run off?

fine be that way

not the first time you suddenly left

guessing it won't be the last

11:24 PM

Dorian: hey tris

I know you're in bed

I just wanted to say that I'm sorry

I let my anger and frustration get the better of me

I shouldn't have done that

hope you see these in the morning and still want to talk to me

but I get it if you don't

13 *Our Place*

Friday, September 21, 4:31 PM

Tristan: Hi, Dorian.

Thanks for the apology.

Dorian: hey tris

again I'm really sorry

I was kind of a dick last night

Tristan: Yeah, you were.

Dorian: I shouldn't have said all that

I went back and read it

I don't resent you tris

and I hate that I came off that way

Tristan: It's fine, Dorian. I understand.

I hurt you. Even though I didn't mean to, it still made you upset.

Dorian: no

I was the dick here

you can't steal my apology

Tristan: I can and I will.

Dorian: so can we talk about yesterday without you getting mad?

Tristan: Why would I get mad?

Dorian: you got kinda pissy last night

Tristan: Pissy?

Dorian: tris

when you type one word answers I know something is up

I know I can't see your face and we're talking online and everything but you do an awful job hiding your emotions

why were you upset?

Tristan: I dunno . . .

I guess I didn't like that you were getting angry at me for trying to help.

Dorian: it really means that much to you that I talk to aj?

Tristan: Well, yeah.

Dorian: despite the fact that the last time I tried that it became a fight?

Tristan: Did you tell him the whole truth the last time?

Dorian: I talked to him

Tristan: But you kept stuff from him. You only told him half the story.

Dorian: I suppose

would you be happier if I "told the whole story"?

Tristan: Yes.

Dorian: ok

I will

Tristan: Really?

Dorian: you don't get it yet do you?

I'd do anything to make you happy tris

Tristan: Dorian . . .

Dorian: I'm not kidding

you're important to me

and if I can make you happy by doing something that easy who am I to say no?

Tristan: Thanks.

Dorian: you're welcome

now can we watch our damn show before it gets spoiled for me?

because it's killing me tristan

literally killing me

I am slowly dying by the minute

Tristan: I don't think it's literally killing you, Dorian.

Dorian: it is

every moment is one moment closer to death

Tristan: You're so morbid!

Dorian: my heart

it hurts

the pain

Tristan: Shut up, you drama queen!

Dorian: was that a crack at me being gay?

Tristan: No, you idiot! That was me telling you to stop your bellyaching and load the damn episode!

Dorian: it's loaded

ready?

Tristan: Play.

Tristan: That was awesome! I can't wait for next week's episode!!

Dorian: same

Tristan: So . . . are you doing boardgames tonight?

Dorian: not sure yet

I think I'm gonna call aj

I'll let you know what happens

Tristan: Okay. Good luck, Dorian.

Dorian: thanks

night

x

Tristan: Bye!

10:49 PM

Dorian: heeeeyyyyyy

Tristan: Are you drunk again, Dorian?

Dorian: lol yaaaaaa i am

hows my tristris

Tristan: I'm fine. Are you okay? Things okay with you and AJ?

Dorian: mooooore than ok!!!!1

i told him im gay

just like uou asked!!!

Tristan: Ahahaha. And?

Dorian: he didny really care which is gooood

Tristan: That's great!

You should probably drink some water and go to bed, though.

Dorian: naaaaah

not when ive got my trisssss

Tristan: Ahaha. Okay, I'll stay for a bit.

Dorian: trissssss

do you think its weird we dont know eachothers names or faces
or stuff?

Tristan: I mean, I guess. A bit.

Dorian: we shoulf!!!

Tristan: Honestly, I kind of like this. I know it's strange, but I feel
a bit safer with us being Dorian and Tristan.

This is our place. Outside, in the real world, I'm that person with
that name. In here? I'm Tristan. I get to be me, exactly as I want
to be.

You know?

Dorian: no im waaaay too drunk for that

im sooorry

Tristan: Ahaha, ten cents.

Dorian: nooooooooo!!!!!

trissss

Tristan: Yes, Dorian?

Dorian: i wanna kiss you

Tristan: Ahaha, yes, Dorian. I know.

Dorian: and i wanna make out with uou

Tristan: Okay Dorian. Settle down.

Dorian: noooo we should do it again i liked thst

Tristan: Yeah, no. Not while you're drunk. Absolutely not.

Dorian: whyyyyyyyyyy

Tristan: I don't really want it to be a thing we do when you drink.
It should be . . . I dunno . . . intimate?
Not to mention that while you may be turned on right now, I most definitely am not.

Dorian: i could tirn you onnn

Tristan: Oh, I sincerely doubt that. Your mistyping and difficult to read messages aren't exactly sexy.
Go to bed, Dorian. We'll do that another day.

Dorian: promise??

Tristan: Yes. Happy?

Dorian: yessss

i was kinfa worried youd never want to do that again tris

but i want to be able to do that with uou

Tristan: Ahaha, okay Dorian.

Dorian: cause if i had you in real life I wpuld kiss uou at ebery

abailable opportunity

Tristan: Okay, Dorian. Go to bed.

And drink some water.

Not necessarily in that order.

Dorian: ok

I love uou!!!

trissssssss??

whered uou go?!?!!???

Tristan: I'm here, I'm here.

Just a bit . . . shellshocked is all.

Dorian: lol wat??

Tristan: You know we've never actually said "I love you" to each

other, right?

Dorian: we havent?

well thats stupid why havent we?

Tristan: Because we've barely known each other for three weeks?

Dorian: i do tjough

Tristan: What?

Dorian: love you

i do love uou

Tristan: Can you stop, please?

Dorian: whyyy??

im just sauing my feelinga

Tristan: Yeah, well, I really never imagined any of this happening

while you're drunk. Honestly, it's kind of uncomfortable for me.

Just go to bed, Dorian.

I'm logging off now.

Goodnight.

Dorian: goodnight tris

byeeee!!!!1!!!!

Saturday, September 22, 10:42 AM

Dorian: hey

I'm sorry

I just went through last night's chat

Tristan: Hey

It's fine. The ramblings of a drunk idiot, right?

Dor?

Dorian: I meant what I said

Tristan: What?

Dorian: I meant what I said tris

Tristan: Dorian, are you sure now is the time to do this?

Dorian: why not?

it's out of the bag

why not tell you properly?

I was kind of tactless

but it was honest

Tristan: Why not? Because you're probably hung-over. I'm kind of
tired. It's been a long week for both of us.

Dorian: it has hasn't it

I thought I lost you this week tris

Tristan: But you didn't. I'm right here.

Dorian: I know

and I'd like you to stay here

Tristan: I will, Dor. Don't worry.

Dorian: ok good

Tristan: So how was boardgame night? Did things go well with AJ?

Dorian: ya actually

things went great

I told him everything

about me being jealous

about me being gay

about you

Tristan: How did he take it?

Dorian: well he thinks it's weird

you and I . . . since we haven't met each other irl yet

but he's trying to be supportive

Tristan: So . . .

He doesn't approve of us?

Dorian: I didn't say that

I think he just needs time to get used to it

I think you and me going only by nicknames weirds him out

but we can keep doing that

your reasoning makes sense

Tristan: Thanks for understanding.

So the games were fun?

Dorian: really fun ya

we ended up talking a lot and drinking

I ended up just telling bambi and spud and they were also super

cool with it

I think each time I tell someone it gets a little easier y'know?

lol bambi even offered to introduce me to a friend of hers

of course I said no

Tristan: Are you sure you wouldn't be happier with a guy who you can be with in real life?

Especially now that you're officially out of the closet?

Dorian: what?

of course not

firstly I wouldn't be out if it wasn't for you

you gave me the courage I needed

secondly I've never felt this way before

you make me so happy tris

and there is no one else that I want to be with in real life or cyberspace

so bambi's friend can suck it

just not mine

Tristan: Thanks, Dor. That's really sweet.

Dorian: it's the truth

what're you up to today?

Tristan: I'm supposed to have my friend over.

Dorian: rose?

Tristan: Yeah.

I just . . . I don't have the energy for it

With all the stress from this week, I just don't have it in me to socialize.

Dorian: can you tell rose you're not up to hanging out?

Tristan: I could. But she's been having a rough time recently, apparently her boyfriend's roommate hates her.

Anyway, I want to be there for her.

Dorian: you know you need to look out for yourself too right?

Tristan: Yeah, I know.

Dorian: shit

I have to go to work

if you don't want rose over tell her

communication

I learned it from you

Tristan: Thanks for the advice. See you tonight, Dor.

Dorian: see you

X

14

Saturday, September 22, 7:14 PM

Dorian: back

Tristan: How was work?

Dorian: fine

aj and bambi came in near the end of my shift

Tristan: I'm glad you're finally getting along with her.

Dorian: same

how was hanging with rose?

Tristan: Pretty funny, actually. She wanted to set me up. Says I've been single for too long.

Dorian: what did you say?

Tristan: I said no. What else would I say?

Dorian: did you tell her about me?

Tristan: Sort of. I didn't tell her that we met on RandoChat . . .

I said we met through online dating.

eSymphony or something.

Dorian: as long as she knows you're not on the market

cause you're not

you're mine

Tristan: Yeah, yeah. She knows. Not single.

Dorian: and she doesn't think it's weird that we haven't met?

Tristan: Not really. I mean, she knows I'm shy and awkward in real life and that I have anxiety. It makes sense for me to date a guy I met online.

Dorian: oh

Tristan: "Oh"?

Dorian: ya

oh

Tristan: "Oh" as in . . . ?

Dorian: as in "oh does that mean you won't ever want to see me irl?"

Tristan: What? No! Of course not!

It just means this is a much easier way for me to get to know someone!

If we had met in real life first, it would have taken a lot longer for me to fall for you.

But chatting online with you? Dor, being around you doesn't take any energy. It just . . . feels right. And I think that's easier because I get to chat with you via text.

Does that make sense?

Dorian: ya

I get it

so

you would still want to meet me one day right?

Tristan: Yeah, of course.

One day.

But this is what I need for now.

Dorian: that's cool

I'm patient

I'll just have to find someone else to have sex with in the meantime

Tristan: Jerk.

Dorian: oh come on

you know I'm kidding

hey tris

Tristan: Yeah?

Dorian: speaking of sex . . .

Tristan: Subtle.

Dorian: what?

can I help it that speaking to my boyfriend makes me horny?

Tristan: Yes. Yes, you can.

Dorian: come on

you were into it last week

Tristan: Ugh, don't remind me. It was so embarrassing.

Dorian: why? It was hot

Tristan: Ahahaha

Dorian: we don't have to do anything you don't want to

hey tris . . .

Tristan: Yeah?

Dorian: let me know if I ever say anything to make you uncomfortable ok?

Tristan: Okay.

Dorian: I'm serious about this

anything at all

I know gender dysphoria can be hard. I just don't want to say anything that might make it worse

Tristan: Wow. You did your research! Yeah, thanks. I'll let you know if you say anything I'm not comfortable with.

Dorian: I just wanted to make sure I understood everything as much as I could in case you needed someone to talk to

Tristan: Thanks, Dor.

Dorian: no problem

Tristan: Hey . . . Do you wanna try voice chat again?

Dorian: sure

You have started a voice chat with Dorian.

Voice chat with Dorian has ended.

Dorian: I love you.

you don't have to say it back

but I know what I'm feeling

and I'm in love

hey . . . tris?

Tristan: Yeah?

Dorian: thanks for that

I needed it

Tristan: Ahaha, you're welcome.

It's not like it was a one-sided thing.

I enjoyed it too.

Dorian: good

I'm glad

Tristan: Getting kinda sleepy . . .

Dorian: yeah

same

go to bed

get some rest

I'll see you tomorrow

Tristan: G'night Dor.

Dorian: night tris

X

Sunday, September 23, 11:02 AM

Dorian: morning

Tristan: Good morning, Dorian.

Dorian: glad you're still here

Tristan: What do you mean?

Dorian: last time we did what we did last night you ran away for a few days

Tristan: Fine. Want me to leave? I have no problem going.

Dorian: then who will watch basker with me tomorrow?

Tristan: Maybe Bambi will. You should ask her.

Dorian: ya maybe I will

she can bring that guy she wants to set me up with

Tristan: As if he'd want to be with you. You're a total nerd.

Dorian: good point

guess I'm just stuck with you

lol

Tristan: Haha.

Got any plans for today?

Dorian: not much

just work

Tristan: What time do you work?

Dorian: noon

Tristan: Aw, that's so soon.

Dorian: is my tristan gonna miss me?

that's a new one

Tristan: Don't flatter yourself. You're just the only person who wants to talk to me.

Dorian: fair enough

guess you scared rose off when you told her you didn't want to date her friend

Tristan: Ahaha, possibly.

Guess whoever she knows must be pretty desperate to date a guy he's never met before.

Dorian: lol imagine that

dating someone you've never even seen before . . .

Tristan: Ahahaha

Dorian: ok g2g

talk to you when I get back

X

Tristan: Bye!

7:09 PM

Dorian: back

Tristan: Welcome back.

How was work?

Dorian: it was fine

do anything exciting while I was gone?

Tristan: Yeah, actually. I went on this site called RandoChat and met this guy there. And now we're dating. Sorry about that. Guess you'll have to go find someone else.

Dorian: oh damn

and just when I thought things were getting serious

guess I'll have to give this engagement ring to someone else

I'll ask bambi if her friend is still available

Tristan: You'd better be joking about that ring, because I am NOT saying yes to you. Not until I have at least five dollars in the jar.

Dorian: well what are you waiting for?

start apologizing

Tristan: I'm sorry, I'm sorry, I'm sorry, I'm sorry.

Dorian: lol

you're such a dork

I love you

shit

that one slipped out

Tristan: It's fine

Dorian: no it's not

I know you're not ready for that

I have to respect that

sorry

Tristan: Ten cents.

Dorian: ya I'll just mail that to you right now

what's your address again?

Tristan: 123 Woeful Victim of Stalkers Lane, Ontario, Canada

Dorian: cool

one dime is on its way

oh speaking of hapless stalker victims . . .

Tristan: Where is that sentence going?!

Dorian: aj mentioned that he still wants to meet you

he just wants to make sure you're real I think

Tristan: I feel pretty real . . .

Dorian: lol

dork

Tristan: Shoot, it's getting kinda late.

I'll talk to you tomorrow, yeah?

Dorian: of course

Tristan: Night!

Dorian: night tris

x

15 Chance Meeting

Monday, September 24, 4:58 PM

Alex arrived at the coffee shop fifteen minutes early. Alex arrived everywhere fifteen minutes early. He hated being late. It gave him a lot of time to read whatever book he was carrying around in his bag.

Alex closed his eyes for a moment and took a deep breath. He hoped beyond hope that Jake Greenspan wouldn't pull a Daisy Chan and make him wait for over half an hour. Daisy, Alex's oldest friend and the one he referred to online as Rose, was always late.

Alex was only part way through the first chapter of his book when he heard a familiar voice.

"Yeah, I'll see you at home, man. Gotta meet with a classmate."

Alex snapped his book shut as his head shot up and his shoulders tensed.

Alex had never seen his classmate outside of school, but now he noticed subtle details that he hadn't picked up on before. Jake's sunglasses half hid eyes that seemed to flicker across the room, searching. His prominent jawline was broken up by an easy smile and subtle laugh lines. He had dark stubble on pale skin, a strong contrast Alex could see from across the room. The multiple earrings in each ear sparkled in the light.

Most importantly, Jake Greenspan had long hair.

Alex had almost forgotten how attractive he found long hair on a man. Jake smacked him in the face with a blatant reminder. It took every bit of strength Alex had not to stare as Jake's black-painted fingernails wove in and out of the silky locks.

Then Jake saw Alex.

Alex looked away, feeling the heat brewing in his cheeks. He busied himself digging through his bag, pretending to search for his notebook and pencil. What was *wrong* with him? Why was Jake suddenly so much more attractive? Alex mentally scolded himself, knowing that he never used to get distracted by boys like that. Not before Dorian.

"Hey."

Alex looked up to see a wry grin spread across Jake's frustratingly handsome face.

"Hello," Alex muttered. He sat straighter and gripped a pencil tightly in his hand.

"How do you take your coffee?" Jake asked.

Alex raised his brow at the question, finding it a little hard to think clearly.

Jake's smile grew wider. "Coffee. It's a coffee shop. I'm gonna grab some. How do you take yours?"

"Oh . . ." Alex thought for a moment. He had

to pull himself back to reality and away from Jake's startling eyes. "Um . . . milk and a bit of cinnamon." He noticed Jake's eyes glance down and back up, his smile growing wider and softer by the moment.

"Unusual." There was something odd about Jake's tone — something Alex didn't recognize. "I like it. One coffee with milk and cinnamon, coming right up. I'll be right back."

In an instant, Alex was left staring at the back of Jake Greenspan's leather jacket and wondering about the interaction they had just had. This was a very different Jake than Alex had expected based on their conversations in class.

As Jake ordered their drinks, Alex reached into his bag and pulled out his laptop. He placed it carefully on the wobbly table. As he bent down to plug it in, he saw a pair of Doc Martens appear before him. From above his head came a joyful laugh.

"Whatya doing down there?"

Alex sat up and straightened his sweater before answering. "Laptop's old. It doesn't have a good battery life." It was a boring response, and Alex knew his ears must be glowing with embarrassment. He looked up at Jake to gauge his reaction and immediately regretted it.

Jake was sitting on the table. He grinned and ran a hand lazily through his hair. Alex had never thought of himself as having a fondness for "bad boys." But there was something about Jake that made his chest tighten and his stomach do somersaults.

"Ready?" Jake's smile didn't fade as he handed a coffee cup to Alex, who carefully took it with a muttered, "Thank you."

Jake laughed again before hopping off the table and sitting in the chair across from his partner. "Are you ready to work on the assignment, Alex?"

Alex swallowed. Hard. The way Jake said his name was insanely charming. "Uh . . . yeah. Ready."

"Good!" Jake pulled out a laptop of his own and set it on the table. "So I like what we've got so far, but I think we can do better . . ."

Alex watched as Jake's fingers danced across the keys, and listened as he talked, with his rich as honey voice, about his ideas for the project. Alex brought his coffee to his lips and took a sip, hoping to calm himself with a bit of caffeine and a pause. When he set the coffee down, Alex focused on his own computer. Maybe avoiding Jake's bold stare would help him concentrate on the work they had to do.

"What do you think of what I wrote?" Jake asked as Alex eyed the computer screen.

"*Alex?*" The woman's voice came from across the room. It sounded excited and curious all at once.

Alex felt his heart jump into his throat, as it beat so fast he feared he might need CPR. He looked up to find Daisy, hand in hand with a man he figured must be her boyfriend.

"Alex! That *is* you! What the hell are you doing here?!"

"Uh ... English?" It was the only answer that Alex could come up with. Daisy's boyfriend punched Jake in the arm playfully and said something that Alex, in his state of shock, didn't listen to. Instead, he just stared at Daisy, slack-jawed and utterly confused.

Daisy pulled the table beside Alex's closer and sat down, beaming brightly at him. "Alex, this is Arjun! Arjun, this is my friend Alex!"

"Hey!" Arjun nodded politely at Alex as he pulled up his own chair and sat down across from Daisy, next to Jake.

"And, Alex, it seems like you've already met Arjun's roommate Jake!" Daisy smiled gently at Jake, who nodded in her direction. The look on Daisy's face changed to a sly smirk as she lowered her voice and leaned closer to Alex. "You know, Alex," she said, their cheeks nearly touching, "This is the guy I wanted to set you up with. I see you're already *on* a date, though! Good for —"

Alex pulled away. He sat straighter and fiddled with the hem of his sweater. "We're here for a project, Daisy. We're in the same class. *Classmates*. That's all. We have an assignment."

Jake and Arjun both looked over.

Alex realized he must have sounded more defensive than he meant to. He snapped his laptop closed and began shoving his things into his bag. "But you guys look like you want to socialize," he said. "Which is fine. I should go anyway. Don't want to interrupt."

Jake stared at Alex with concern. "You don't want to keep working on the assignment? We can tell these two to leave us alone for a bit . . ."

"No, no, no, no," Alex sputtered. He tried to shove his laptop into the wrong pocket of his bag. "You stay, I'll go. We can always work on this later, it's not due 'till Wednesday. I'll leave you guys be, don't want to be a hassle . . ."

"*Alex*," Daisy said firmly, putting a hand on her friend's arm. Alex looked up into bright brown eyes filled with worry. Daisy took a deep breath and gave her friend an affectionate smile. "Alex, you should stay. You have an assignment to do. School should come first. Arjun and I will join Jake after."

"But —" Alex began, before Jake's voice cut him off.

"It's okay, Alex, if you don't want to stay." Jake's voice was soft and steady and full of understanding. "We can meet tomorrow in the library. It's a bit more private there. Fewer . . . *interruptions*." Jake shot his roommate a dirty look before turning back to his classmate. A kind smile replaced his usually cocky grin. "How does that sound?"

Alex stared at Jake, trying to make sense of what had just happened. The Jacob Greenspan he had seen in class was so different from this guy, Alex almost couldn't believe they were the same person. Alex glanced over at Daisy, who was still staring anxiously at him. Then over at Arjun, who seemed confused.

With a slight nod, Alex turned back to Jake and smiled for the first time all afternoon.

"Yeah . . . tomorrow. Library. What time?"

"How's noon?"

"Sounds good." Alex grabbed his bag and lifted it onto his shoulder before standing up and turning to his friend and her boyfriend. "See you later, Daisy. Goodbye, Arjun."

"Bye, Alex," said Daisy.

"It was nice to meet you," Arjun offered as Alex walked away.

16 *Attraction*

Monday, September 24, 9:09 PM

Dorian: hey

Tristan: Hey!

Dorian: how was school?

Tristan: Not bad, actually!

How was work?

Dorian: fine

same as usual

any idea what you wanna do tonight?

Tristan: We could watch the TTS movies together if you wanted.

Dorian: that's an idea . . .

Tristan: Yeah, especially since number five is coming out next month.

I always like rewatching them before the next one comes out.

Dorian: dork

Tristan: You know you love it.

Dorian: I do

I've got to download them

I don't own a copy

Tristan: Okay, let me know when the download is ready!

Dorian: will do

Tristan: Hey, Dor . . .

Dorian: ya?

Tristan: I have a weird question.

Dorian: . . .

ok?

Tristan: do you have long hair?

Dorian: lol

you're right

that's a weird question

you've never asked me what I looked like before

but yes I do

why?

Tristan: Oh, I was just thinking about that character from the TTS books, you know? And how he has long hair . . .

And I remembered just how good guys look with long hair . . .

You're right, it was a stupid question. I'm sorry.

Dorian: ten cents

it wasn't stupid

and I'm glad you like long hair

guess I'll keep mine this way for you

Tristan: Ahaha

Dorian: does that mean I get to ask you a question about what you look like?

Tristan: Oh . . . I guess.

Dorian: you don't have to tell me anything you don't want to

I was just teasing

Tristan: No, no . . . it's fine. I mean, you are my boyfriend I suppose. You deserve to know what I look like.

Dorian: how bout just hair colour?

Tristan: Umm . . .

Brown?

Dorian: like a light brown or a dark brown?

Tristan: Pretty dark.

Dorian: cool

now I will stop every dark haired boy I meet and ask them if they're my tristan

Tristan: And I suppose I should do the same with those long haired guys!

Dorian: who knows

we might even live in the same city

Tristan: On the same block, even.

Dorian: with the same neighbours

Tristan: And the same friends!

Dorian: lol can you imagine?

Tristan: No!

Dorian: you know

if you lived beside me

I'd be over every single day

you wouldn't be able to get me to leave

Tristan: Thank god for small miracles then.

Dorian: lol

movie's done downloading btw

has been for a while

I was just having too much fun to tell you

Tristan: Great! Let's watch!

Dorian: ready?

Tristan: Play!

Tristan: I forgot how good that movie was. Don't get me wrong,

it's nothing like the books. But it's still really fun to watch!

Dorian: especially with you

Tristan: You're such a sap!

Shoot, it's getting late. I should head off soon.

Dorian: ok see you tomorrow

Tristan: See you! G'night!

Dorian: night tris

X

Tuesday, September 25, 11:56 AM

Alex entered the library, clinging tightly to his bag,
keeping eyes out for his English partner. He was

determined to be less distracted than the day before. He would buckle down, get some work done and get home. No more soft grey eyes and sharp cheekbones. No more cocky smirks and fingers running through hair. Alex would not stare.

There was a moment when Alex regretted not exchanging numbers with Jake. But those worries were washed away when he heard someone call his name. He turned around to find Jake walking towards him. His knapsack was slung over one shoulder, hair tied back in a loose bun. He was grinning broadly as he nodded and held up a hand in greeting. Alex nodded back and couldn't help but smile. Something about Jake's crooked grin was contagious.

"Hey, Alex."

"Hey."

Alex watched as Jake's eyes scanned the tables, searching for a quiet spot to work. "Oh! There's a spot!"

Alex glanced in the direction that Jake was looking and saw what his classmate was pointing at. Not a table and chairs, but a couch with a coffee table. It wasn't ideal, but it would do.

Alex and Jake headed towards the couch in silence. It seemed smaller up close than it did from the library entrance. Alex swallowed hard. He would be sitting directly next to Jake, shoulder to shoulder, thigh to thigh.

Jake plopped himself down first. He opened his laptop and placed it on his legs. Alex followed suit, plugging in his computer behind the couch and sitting down. Their sides were pressed together and Alex could feel a lump forming in his throat. He took a deep breath and opened the file on his laptop, trying to focus on one thing: English.

"So," Jake started, clearly not fazed by Alex pressing firmly against him. "Wanna go over it from the start?"

"Yeah," Alex agreed as he scrolled to the top. He tried not to notice that Jake smelled like cigarettes and leather, with a hint of cologne that was spicy and rich. It made Alex's stomach tighten.

"Okay," Jake began, "I'll start as Cesario . . ."

Alex watched as Jake's lips moved around the words, barely aware of what they were even saying.

"Alex, it's your turn."

"Oh! Oh, yes. Sorry. Yeah . . . Sorry, one sec."

Ten cents.

Alex tried to clear his thoughts and focus on his Shakespearean dialogue. The two boys continued reading their assignment aloud and adjusting the wording here and there. Then they quickly picked up where they had left off the day before.

The more work they did, the easier it became for Alex to concentrate. English really was interesting, and he found that he was actually learning something in the class. To his surprise, he was also discovering that Jake seemed to enjoy the subject. Counter to Alex's first impression that Jake didn't care about the class, Jake was keen to push himself to write a dialogue that was in-depth and challenging.

It wasn't until Alex felt his stomach rumble that he checked the time. When he realized how long they had been there, he said, "Jake, it's already one! I have to get to class!"

Jake looked up from his computer. He smiled at Alex, tucking a loose strand of black hair behind his ear. "Wow, so it is. I guess time really flies when you're having fun."

"Yeah . . ."

Jake's laptop clicked closed before he stood up. He reached out his hand to Alex, who hesitated for a moment before grasping it and letting Jake help him up. "Go to class, Alex. I'll finish up this last bit and you can look over it tonight."

"Sounds like a plan," Alex answered. He shoved his hands in his pockets and willed his cheeks not to turn red.

"Cool. See you tomorrow then."

"See you." Alex hurriedly packed up his things and threw his bag over his shoulder before heading out. As he walked towards the entrance of the library, he wondered if Jake felt the same spark that he did when their hands had touched.

7:22 PM

Tristan: Hey!

Dorian: hey

how was school?

Tristan: Good. You?

Dorian: kinda fun

I'm starting to really enjoy my classes

Tristan: That's awesome!

Dorian: ya

so any idea what you wanted to do tonight

Tristan: Oh, I had an idea or two . . .

Dorian: go on

You have started a voice chat with Dorian.

Voice chat with Dorian has ended. **Dorian:** so who are you and
what have you done with my tristan?

Tristan: Haha.

I dunno, I guess I was just thinking about you today and needed
some . . . release?

I'm sorry.

Dorian: oh no don't you dare apologize for that

that was amazing

ten cents

Tristan: Ahahaha, okay.

Dorian: tris you're so perfect

dammit I just want to cuddle you to sleep

Tristan: I wouldn't mind that.

Dorian: but it's a little early for sleeping right now

Tristan: I guess, yeah.

We've just never done that and continued chatting before.

Dorian: lol

is that a bad thing?

Tristan: No, I guess not.

It's just weird . . . doing 'it' together, you know. It's a weird thing.

Dorian: I don't think it's weird

it's also the only way we can be intimate if that's what we want

to do

and it's definitely what I want to do

Tristan: I guess. And, I mean, I do enjoy it.

Dorian: good

so do I

Tristan: Okay.

Dorian: lol

glad we could clear that up

now get over here so we can watch a movie or something

Tristan: All right. Timetale Series 2?

Dorian: I'd never say no to more tts

ready?

Tristan: Yeah. Play.

Dorian: I wish I had that ability . . .

Tristan: What, time travel?

Dorian: no just stopping time

I don't need to travel in it

I'd be good just pausing it

Tristan: I know what you mean.

All the good moments would last a bit longer.

Dorian: exactly . . .

Tristan: I like the second movie!

Dorian: me too

but the third is my favourite

Tristan: Same!

Okay, getting kinda sleepy. Gonna head off.

Goodnight, Dorian. :)

Dorian: good night tris

x

17 Double Vision

Wednesday, September 26, 8:25 AM

Alex was running late for class.

He wasn't really running late, but in his mind, not being ten minutes early was as good as being late. And on Wednesday, Alex was only five minutes early for English class.

By the time he entered the classroom, there was already a scattering of students. Alex kept his head down and paid them no attention until he realized that one of those students was sitting in the chair next to his usual seat.

The first thing Alex noticed were the Doc Martens. Alex's heart skipped a beat. He forced his eyes up to meet the silvery eyes that he couldn't seem to shake from his mind.

Jake smiled softly at Alex and nodded in greeting.

Alex swallowed. He could feel his chest tighten and his heart hammer against his ribcage, threatening to explode at any moment. He forced himself to smile and nod, still standing awkwardly beside his chair.

"Morning, Alex," Jake offered. He seemed to enjoy the state of panic he was inducing in Alex. He ran a hand through his dark hair and leaned back in his chair as if he didn't have a single worry in the world.

"Morning," Alex mumbled in response. He placed his bag on the ground and awkwardly tried to insert himself into the uncomfortable chair-desk hybrid that he hated.

"I printed off the assignment and put it on Hammond's desk." Jake inclined his head towards the teacher's desk, where a copy of their dialogue sat. "You did a great job on that, by the way. I was surprised."

"You were . . ." Alex was taken aback by Jake's words. "Why were you surprised?"

Jake chuckled softly. His shoulders rose and fell, making the zippers on his jacket rattle. "English just didn't seem like your kind of subject. Guess I was wrong."

Alex opened his mouth to argue, to defend himself. To get angry at Jake for underestimating him. But the sound of the teacher's voice interrupted his thoughts.

"Good morning, class!"

Alex closed his mouth and shot Jake an angry glare. Then he turned to face the front of the classroom.

Mr. Hammond pulled a stack of papers from his briefcase and turned to the class with a broad smile. "Now that we have all the dialogues in, it's time for assignment two!"

The teacher handed Jake the stack of paper and returned to the front of the class. Jake grabbed a copy for himself, placed one on Alex's desk and passed the stack back to the student behind him.

"Today we will continue our readings on *Twelfth Night*. For your assignment, you will be getting into pairs and presenting . . ."

Alex felt a nudge from the left and turned to look at Jake, who had a smirk creeping across his lips.

"Wanna be my partner?" Alex felt his stomach tighten. He found the idea of being partnered with Jake again surprisingly exciting.

Alex smiled and nodded as Jake grinned at him. Jake turned back to face the teacher, a slight redness spreading across his pale face. Alex's eyes darted down to the assignment sheet in front of him as he tried not to let his own embarrassment show.

The class continued as Hammond talked about Shakespeare. Alex was scribbling notes in his book, writing everything his teacher said.

Every once in a while, Jake would lean in, peek and make a joking comment about the state of Alex's writing. "I'm surprised you can even read that," Jake teased. The smell of cigarettes and leather filled the air around Alex. "What does that even say?"

Alex rolled his eyes, but he couldn't keep the smile from his lips. "At least I'm taking notes. Remind me again why I agreed to be your partner?"

Jake laughed quietly and leaned back. "I learn by listening, Alex. You can't fault me for my learning style."

Alex raised an eyebrow and shook his head, his smile growing wider. "Can I fault you for your fashion style, then?"

Jake's laugh was loud enough to earn him a look from the teacher. "Who are you kidding? You love it!" Jake said under his breath.

Alex felt his cheeks get warm and returned his focus to the page. He tried to listen to what Hammond was saying, but his mind kept wandering. The playful bickering he was having with Jake felt familiar. Discomfort settled in the pit of Alex's stomach, eating at him from the inside. Alex felt guilty, knowing that his banter with Jake wasn't as innocent as he tried to convince himself it was.

Alex reminded himself about Dorian. His *boyfriend*, the man he had fallen for on the other side of the computer screen. He tried to focus on his memory of their words and their jokes and the things they talked about. In his mind, Jake's voice even sounded a little like Dorian's. But it was hard to tell because all he heard was a breathy whisper when he and Dorian actually talked.

I'm sorry, Dor, Alex thought.

Alex's grip tightened on his pencil as he realized the face floating through his mind was Jake's. It was his classmate's face that he went to when he tried to imagine *Dorian*.

"*Ten cents*," imaginary Jake said, that smug half-smirk on his face.

Alex felt another nudge from his left and turned to face Jake.

Jake looked slightly confused. "You're not gonna write that down? Isn't this important?"

Alex blinked. He blinked again. He looked down at his page and realized he hadn't been taking notes. He shrugged, pretending that he wasn't worried. "I'm sure

I can figure it out later."

Jake smiled and rolled his eyes. "So much for note taking."

By the time the class ended, Alex felt tension he could cut with a knife. As soon as the teacher dismissed them, he practically leaped from his chair. He frantically stuffed his notebook into his bag, which was lying open on the ground.

As Alex crouched, Jake stood up beside him and gave him a gentle poke with his foot. "Hey, you busy?"

Alex looked up, his mouth half open, trying to figure out what Jake was asking. "Uh . . . I'm packing my bag?"

Jake laughed and ran a hand through his hair. "I didn't mean literally right now, you dork. I meant, like, after last class. I wanted to know if you wanted to get coffee. Maybe get a head start on our assignment?"

Alex felt his face flush and looked down to stare intently at the zipper he was struggling with.

It was just coffee. It was just an assignment. Why did it feel so wrong?

"So . . . ?" Jake asked.

Alex looked up again, slightly dismayed that Jake was still standing there. He hoped that maybe his own awkwardness had scared off his classmate. "Uh . . . I shouldn't. I'm sorry. I've got . . . I have things to do . . . I'm sorry."

Ten cents.

Jake offered Alex his hand. Alex hesitated before he grabbed it and let Jake help him to his feet.

Jake laughed again. "What, your girlfriend is waiting for you or something?"

"*What*? No! I don't . . . I mean . . . no! I don't have a girlfriend . . . or anything. No one is waiting. I just . . . there are things . . ." Alex's words trailed off into a mumble as Jake continued to laugh.

"It's fine. We'll work on our assignment another time. Here . . ." Jake handed his phone to Alex. Alex held it in his hands, unsure of what to do with it. Was it for him?

"Put your number in it!" Jake said.

"Right. Yes. My number. So we can contact each other . . ."

"Yes," Jake said slowly. He raised an eyebrow at Alex. "So we can meet up? For the assignment?"

"Right. Yes. Assignment."

Alex added himself to the contacts before forcing the phone back into Jake's hands. Jake opened his mouth to say something, but Alex quickly turned around. "Okay, gotta go. Sorry, Jake. I'll see you around!"

Alex practically ran for the classroom door. The last thing he heard from Jake was a very confused "goodbye."

18 Meeting Cute

Wednesday, September 26, 8:32 PM

Dorian: hey tris

Tristan: Hey.

Dorian: how was school today?

Tristan: Good.

Dorian: even that class with the kid you hate?

Tristan: Yeah. He's actually not as awful as I used to think. He's kind of a good guy.

Dorian: that's good to hear

Tristan: How were your classes?

Dorian: great

I'm really enjoying them

Tristan: Not too much, I hope?

Dorian: never

lol

so abrupt change of subject

wanna meet aj?

it doesn't have to be right now

Tristan: Yeah, I'd love to meet him at some point. Now just seems

a little soon?

Dorian: fair enough

how about tomorrow?

Tristan: Sure . . .

Dorian: there's nothing to be afraid of

aj is a cool guy

Tristan: I'm not afraid.

Well, not exactly.

I just . . . I don't want to "meet" him and then he hates me. What

would I do if your best friend hated me?

Dorian: ok firstly he won't hate you

that's literally impossible

because you're amazing

Tristan: Dor . . .

Dorian: secondly

even if we were in an alternate universe where he hated you

I'd tell him to buzz off

he's my best friend

so that means he has to learn to like you, whether or not he

wants to

Tristan: You're such a hypocrite. What about Bambi?

Dorian: what?

I'm nice to bambi

we even had coffee together the other day

so ha

Tristan: Was AJ with you?

Dorian: ya

so?

Tristan: So that doesn't count! You haven't hung out with her

one-on-one.

Dorian: baby steps tris

baby steps . . .

Tristan: You're ridiculous.

Dorian: hey!

Tristan: No, it's endearing. I love it.

Dorian: excellent

I'll keep it up then

Tristan: So, how do you wanna go about me meeting AJ?

It's not like we can bump into each other in a coffee shop or something.

Dorian: I figured we could just start a group chat and go from there

Tristan: Okay, that sounds like a good idea.

Dorian: so . . .

complete change of subject again

wanna know what I just realized today

Tristan: What?

Dorian: we're complete idiots

Tristan: You just realized that?

Dorian: yup

Tristan: Okay, what brought on this realization?

Dorian: we forgot to watch basker on monday

Tristan: Oh my god!!

How? What were we doing Monday that made us both forget?!

Dorian: uh . . . we talked on here

we watched tts

I had work that afternoon

Tristan: Oh! I remember now.

I met with my classmate at school that day. I must have been super distracted because of the assignment and everything.

Dorian: wanna watch it now?

Tristan: Sure!

Lemme download it.

Dorian: ya I gotta do the same

ready?

Tristan: Play!

Dorian: ok I liked that episode

Tristan: Same!

Dorian: they did a good job setting things up for when the boys meet

dropping little hints here and there

I'm kind of excited for next monday

Tristan: Me too.

Dorian: shoot

aj is calling me

talk to you tomorrow

Tristan: Night!

Dorian: night

x

Thursday, September 27, 5:02 PM

Tristan: Hey!

Dorian: hey tris

Sorry for ditching you last night.

Tristan: Oh, it's totally fine! You have a life outside of here!

Dorian: lol

so . . .

you ready?

Tristan: For . . . ?

Dorian: to meet aj

Tristan: Oh. No, not really.

Dorian: it'll be fine

he'll love you I promise

how can he not?

Tristan: Yeah . . .

Sure . . .

Dorian: you've got this tristan

Tristan: Okay, let's get this over with.

Dorian: ok, lemme set up a group chat

hang on

AyyJay has joined the chat.

Tristan: Hello, AJ! It's nice to finally meet you! I've heard a lot about you!

AyyJay: hey tristan

same

dorian wont shut up about u

Tristan: Ahahaha, I hope you've only heard good things!

AyyJay: nah dorian wouldnt talk crap abt u

not if he knows whats good for him

Tristan: Ahaha!

AyyJay: hey can my girlfriend join

?

shes veen dying to meet the infamous tristan thst dorian keeps talking about

Tristan: Sure!

Dorian: fine . . .

AyyJay: thx

kk

gimme a sec

Tristan: Okay!

Flora has joined the chat

Flora: Hello!

AyyJay: hey babe

Tristan: Oh! This must be the Bambi I've heard so much about!

Flora: Bambi?

Tristan: Ahaha, yeah. Dorian's never given me a name to call you.
He said you had big fawn eyes, something AyyJay pointed out. So
now we just call you Bambi.

Flora: Aww! That's kind of sweet!

AyyJay: lol

Tristan: So . . .

What can I call you, Miss Bambi? I'm guessing Flora?

Flora: lol, yeah! My mom and I are really into flowers, so I thought
Flora suited me!

Tristan: That's cool!

Flora: So, Tristan, what do you do?

Tristan: Well, I'm a student and I like video games and stuff.

I watch a lot of TV. Lately Dorian and I have been watching our favourite shows together.

Dorian: lol you make me sound like such a nerd

Flora: That's really cool! 😊

Tristan: How about you guys? Are you in school?

Flora: We're both at the same university!

Tristan: That's cool! What do you study?

Flora: I'm in bio and AJ is in business.

AyyJay: can i just say . . .

tristan

youve rlly helped dorian mellow out since meeting u

Dorian: what the hell is that supposed to mean?

AyyJay: it means i think Tristan is perfect for u

and im happy u found him

Dorian: oh

ok

thanks

Tristan: And honestly, I think you and Flora make a cute couple, too!

Flora: Awww!! Thanks Tristan!! 😊

Dorian: cool

you all met

everyone happy now?

can we get back to our regularly scheduled programming?

Tristan: You mean watching TV and movies and complaining about inconsistencies in canon?

Flora: lol! Is that what you guys do, Dorian?! 😁

Dorian: well

it's not all we do

AyyJay: ew

stop

ive herd enough

Dorian: I didn't mean that perv

we just chat about life and shit

AyyJay: this is a side of dorian ive never seen before

im imoressed

*impressed

Flora: lol! I've gotta say, I am too! I haven't known Dorian for very long, but he told me Tristan's the reason he actually started talking to me. So, thank you! 😊

Tristan: Oh, he mentioned that?

Flora: Yeah! You've had quite the impact on him, apparently! 😊

AyyJay: k

i approve

u can keep dating him dorian

no creepy stalker would put up with u for that long

not if it wasnt love

Dorian: lol

thanks?

AyyJay: dont mention it

k im off

flora and i have a date

c u later

Flora: It was nice meeting you, Tristan! 😊

Tristan: Likewise!

Goodnight!

Flora: Night! 😴

AyyJay: bye

AyyJay has left the chat.

Flora has left the chat.

Dorian: see?

that wasn't so bad

I'm glad you met

and I'm glad he likes you

makes me feel like you and I totally made the right decision to date

date

Tristan: I think we did.

Dorian: love you tris

now let's watch some tv

Tristan: Um . . . I should go soon.

It's getting kinda late and I have class tomorrow and everything.

Dorian: oh

ok . . .

you alright?

Tristan: Yeah, I'm fine.

Dorian: you sure?

you seem a bit off

Tristan: Don't worry, it's fine. Just tired is all.

I'll see you tomorrow.

Dorian: ok

goodnight

Tristan: Bye

Dorian: x

19 *Crush*

Friday, September 28, 4:09 PM

Alex regretted his decision to grab a coffee with Daisy the moment she told him where they were headed.

"Let's go to the Moondoe near your school," she grinned as she led the way.

Alex froze in his tracks and tried to think of an excuse. But Daisy looped her arm through his and practically dragged him towards the coffee shop.

"Daisy . . ." Alex protested when they were a block

away from the coffee shop he had been dreaming about since Monday. "This is where Jake hangs out."

"Yeah, so?" Daisy looked at Alex and cocked an eyebrow. Alex watched as she chewed her lip and tried to read him. "It's not as if you like him or anything. You have a boyfriend, remember?"

Alex caught himself before he looked down at his feet. Instead he chose to focus intently ahead of him. It took every ounce of strength he could muster to keep his expression calm. "Of course I don't like him, Daisy. Don't be ridiculous." Alex made a point of rolling his eyes. "I just don't want to bump into a classmate outside of school if I don't have to."

Daisy let out a chuckle and gave Alex's arm a gentle squeeze. "You really need to get out more, Alex. Not everyone at school is gonna bite, you know."

She pulled him into the coffee shop, where Alex avoided eye contact with everyone in the room. Daisy went to the counter to order their drinks and Alex made a beeline for a table in the corner, the one farthest from other people he could find. When Daisy sat down with their coffees, Alex's leg was bouncing up and down and his hands were tapping nervously against the table.

"What is with you today, Alex? You're acting . . . different." Daisy sounded concerned as she reached out and put a hand on Alex's.

"I . . . I just . . ." Alex had to think quickly and come up with a reasonable excuse. "I have a group project due soon and it's stressing me out . . ."

Daisy narrowed her eyes at her friend.

"I'm partnered with Jake."

"Ah. Yeah, that makes sense." Daisy broke into a smile and tucked a strand of purple hair behind her ear. "Jake doesn't seem the type to put in a lot of effort for group projects."

"Exactly," Alex lied. He wrapped his fingers around his coffee cup, hoping it could somehow teleport him to anywhere else in the world. "So I didn't really want to bump into him."

"Oh . . ." Daisy looked down, swirling her coffee in its paper cup. "Guess that answers my next question."

"Your next question?" Alex glared at Daisy. He knew the look she got when she was attempting to force him to socialize.

"Yeah . . . Arjun is having some friends over tonight. I thought it would be nice if you joined us. He said it's okay. He's making curry." From her tone, Daisy seemed to think homemade curry would be the deciding factor for Alex. It wasn't.

"Thanks for the offer," Alex mumbled politely. He kept himself from telling his friend off. "But I'd rather stay home."

Daisy shifted in her chair. Alex could feel her eyes digging into him, even as he kept his focus on his coffee.

"You really should —"

"I don't need your help to make friends, Daisy," Alex said sharply. "I'm not that lost little boy you met in middle school."

Silence fell over their table. The dull background noise of the coffee shop filled the void as Alex and Daisy stared at their drinks.

It took a few moments, but Daisy eventually spoke up. "I know you're not that person anymore, Alex." She took a steadying breath before looking up to capture Alex's eyes with her own. "But I worry about you. You never go out. You never talk to people."

"I have my boyfriend."

"Yes, yes. The guy you met on eSymphony whose name you won't tell me. The same guy you haven't met in real life yet because you'd prefer to keep things safe. Is that the boyfriend you're talking about?"

Alex didn't respond.

"Look, I think you should join us tonight. It would be good for you."

Alex thought about standing up, leaving the table. Letting Daisy sit by herself and drink alone. Instead, he looked directly at his friend, took a deep breath and spoke his mind. "I said 'no thank you,' Daisy. I'd appreciate it if you respected that. I don't have the energy to socialize right now and I need you to understand that I know my own limits."

"Okay. I'm sorry."

Alex's heart ached for his friend as he saw her face fall. The excitement that had been bubbling out of her faded entirely. "It's fine," Alex said calmly. "I just don't really want to spend a whole evening with —"

"*Jake?*"

Alex froze, hoping beyond hope that Daisy was finishing his sentence. As the smell of cigarettes, leather and spiced cologne filled his nose and made his head swim, Alex knew he was in trouble.

"Hey, Alex," the voice behind him said, low and raspy, almost a soft growl.

Alex inhaled deeply before turning around and facing Jake. "Hey . . ."

The cocky grin, the loose bun, the lopsided backpack. It was all enough to make Alex smile despite himself. Jake grabbed a chair from the table next to theirs and pulled it over. He plopped himself down beside his classmate. He gave Alex the once-over and sized him up before flashing a confident smirk. Alex tried to suppress his blush, willing his cheeks not to give him away.

"So," Jake began, running his fingers through his hair. "I'm guessing Daisy told you about tonight? You game?"

"Thanks, but no thanks," Alex mumbled to his coffee, which didn't respond. "I'm not really one for parties."

"It's not a party, exactly, it's more like —"

"No, *thank you*, Jake." Alex's tone was more forceful than he intended. But he was tired of people trying to pressure him. He was perfectly happy chatting with Dorian before his boardgame night and then watching a movie.

"Oh." Jake's eyes flickered down for a brief moment. His face fell slightly before he recovered. "And there's no way I can convince you otherwise? I'd . . . it'd be really nice if you were there."

Alex's mouth opened on its own, and words spilled out that he didn't intend to say aloud. "Next time, Jake."

The glowing smile on Jake's face was enough to make Alex's knees weak.

A sudden weight dropped into the pit of Alex's stomach. He realized just how smitten he was with his English partner. Almost before he knew what came over himself, Alex was on his feet, throwing his bag over his shoulder. "I have to go."

"*Alex*," Daisy protested. She tried to get her friend to sit down again. "You don't have to come! It's fine! Just sit —"

"I'll see you guys later." Alex turned around, ignoring Daisy's and Jake's words. He refused to look back at the two of them at the table.

Alex needed to go home.

He needed to talk to Dorian.

20 *Feeling Guilty*

Friday, September 28, 5:35 PM

Tristan: I have to talk to you about something, Dorian.

Dorian: ok?

Tristan: You know I love you, right?

Dorian: you have literally never said those words to me before

Tristan: I know.

And I'm sorry.

I do . . .

Love you, that is.

I've had feelings for you since the beginning.

Dorian: hold on tris

let me guess

you've found someone irl that you like

and you want to date them

because you'll have a better chance at having a real relationship

if you can be with them in person

it's obvious

Tristan: I never said that.

Dorian: you didn't have to

I know you tris

I get it

I know that feeling of falling for someone irl

don't get me wrong

I'm angry

but I get it

Tristan: Dorian, would you stop for a second and let me talk, please?

Dorian: I want you to be happy tris

and if that means losing you so be it

that's the worst part about being in love

your happiness is now more important to me than my happiness

Tristan: Let me talk, dammit!

Dorian: fine

what

Tristan: I was going to say that I have a crush on someone.

And I feel ashamed of it.

And I'm sorry!

I don't want to leave you, Dor!

I would never do that to you!

Dammit, I just told you I loved you! Why would I preface a breakup with that?!

I just . . . I wanted to be honest with you.

I didn't want to hide things from my boyfriend.

Dorian: oh

Tristan: Oh?! That's what you have to say?! You made me feel like crap, Dorian! You accused me of wanting to leave you for someone I had met in real life!

And all you have to say is "oh"?!?!

Dorian: I'm sorry

Tristan: You'd better be sorry! I'm sitting here in tears because my boyfriend thinks I'd just up and leave him for someone I'd just met!

Dorian: I'm really sorry tris

you're right

I should have heard you out before getting upset

tristan?

Tristan: Yeah, I'm still here. I'm just angry at you.

Dorian: so . . .

who's this guy you have a crush on?

Tristan: Nobody.

Dorian: tristan please don't shut me out

you were right

honesty is important in a relationship

and I appreciate what you were trying to do

please?

Tristan: He's in my English class.

Dorian: oh?

Tristan: Yeah, he's the guy I thought was annoying at first. We had a project together and . . . he's a lot nicer in person than I thought.

I dunno . . . he reminds me a bit of you.

And it's hard because I can see him, you know?

Dorian: ya I know what you mean

Tristan: And sometimes I just imagine that he's actually you and . . .
And I feel guilty.

Dorian: there's nothing to feel guilty about

that's the thing with emotions, we don't choose who we develop
crushes on

what we do choose is how we act on those feelings

I don't care if you have a crush on someone as long as you don't
go around making out with them

it's just a harmless crush right?

Tristan: I guess . . .

It didn't feel harmless.

Dorian: what does that mean?

Tristan: It means that he's the face I picture whenever I imagine you.

Dorian: ok

now I'm getting kinda jealous

Tristan: Yeah . . .

Dor, I think we should meet.

Dorian: what

Tristan: We don't know what each other looks like. I think that's
stupid, especially since we're dating.

So I think we should meet.

Dorian: jesus tris

it's about goddamn time

I've been trying so hard not to push you or make you uncomfortable

by asking to meet you

but it's been killing me!

Tristan: I had no idea! You never told me!

Dorian: I didn't want to put pressure on you

Tristan: You idiot.

You should have just talked to me about this.

Dorian: ya

I guess I should have

anyways

we should meet

Tristan: Yeah . . .

So I guess the question now is to figure out how far we really are

from each other.

Ontario is a big province.

Dorian: I live in hamilton

it's near toronto-ish

Tristan: Are you messing with me?

Dorian: no?

what?

Tristan: I live in Hamilton too.

Dorian: are you serious?

westdale?

Tristan: Well, yes. This is getting kinda spooky.

Dorian: you're telling me

Tristan: So, when do you want to do this?

Dorian: um . . .

wanna meet on monday at the moondoe at king and paisley?

Tristan: Okay.

Dorian: I'm really excited

Tristan: I'm terrified.

Dorian: there's no reason to be scared!

Tristan: YES THERE IS!

What if we meet and we realize there's no connection in real life?

What if we meet and you're not attracted to me?!

What if we meet and it turns out you've been lying this whole time and you're really just a serial killer?!

Dorian: what if the world exploded tomorrow?

what if there's a pandemic and we're not allowed to meet in person?

you can't dwell on what-ifs tris

you just have to try

and trust that things will work out

Tristan: Easier said than done.

Dorian: dammit

I wish we could talk about this more

but it's boardgame night

Tristan: It's okay. Go play boardgames.

We've got our plan. We're meeting on Monday.

Dorian: ok . . . what time?

Tristan: Um . . . I guess . . . four? Sound good?

Dorian: sounds perfect

Tristan: Tell AJ I say hi.

And we'll talk again tomorrow.

But try not to get too drunk tonight, okay?

Dorian: I make no promises

Tristan: Goodnight, Dor.

Dorian: night tris

I love you

Tristan: Bye.

21 *Can't Wait*

Sunday, September 30, 7:31 PM

Dorian: guess what

Tristan: What?

Dorian: I get to see you tomorrow

Tristan: Yes, I know. Believe it or not, I know my days of the week.

Dorian: you excited?

Tristan: If by "excited" you mean "terrified," then yes. I am.

Dorian: don't be

you know me tris

no matter what happens tomorrow I'm still the same dorian that

I always was

remember that when you see me ok?

Tristan: Okay.

You're making me more nervous, you know. That sounds almost

ominous.

Dorian: I didn't mean for it to sound ominous

I was just hoping it would make you less nervous

it's not like you're meeting me for the first time

we've already gotten to know each other

tomorrow is just gonna be the same as this

only better

Tristan: I guess you're right . . .

Dorian: stop freaking out tris

you're gonna freak me out

Tristan: I'm not freaking out!

Dorian: it's cute

you're saying that as if you think I can't tell

Tristan: Shut up, Dor.

Dorian: okay shutting up

Tristan: So how was work today?

Dorian: honestly?

really hard

Tristan: What? Why?

Dorian: believe it or not I'm anxious too

it's hard to pour hot coffee when your hands are shaking

Tristan: Awww.

So Dorian does have a heart!

Dorian: yup

it's buried somewhere deep down inside

beneath all that bitterness and sarcasm

Tristan: Gonna have to dig real deep for that, aren't I?

Dorian: I mean . . . if you're offering

Tristan: lol

Dorian: ooooh look at that

Tristan is saying lol now

Tristan: Meh . . . it's easier to type.

Dorian: I'm a terrible influence

next you're gonna leave out commas and capital letters

Tristan: Oh dear, you're right. I should stop talking to you so you don't ruin my grammar.

Dorian: good point

we should stop talking to each other on here

Tristan: Wait, really?

Dorian: yeah

starting tomorrow we should just call and text and see each other in person

screw this online chat

I get to have the real tristan

tris?

Tristan: Yeah, I'm here.

I just . . . I don't want to lose this, Dorian.

I don't want anything to change tomorrow just because we meet in person.

If things change, I don't know if I'll be able to handle it.

Dorian: ok

nothing has to change

you keep using your accurate typing

I'll refuse to capitalize

punctuation be damned

nothing has to be different

Tristan: Thanks, Dor.

Dorian: anything for my tristan

hey

let's watch something

to get your mind off of stuff

Tristan: What?

Dorian: tts 3 is next if you wanted to watch that

it's your favourite

Tristan: You're not wrong. I do love that one.

It's the first time they reveal Seith as gay!

God, that was so mind-blowing as a kid, you know? A character in a book who was actually gay? It made such a difference for me growing up.

Dorian: same

it was actually the first time I ever knew that guys could like guys

my parents never let us have anything that mentioned homosexuality at home so I didn't even know it was a thing

good thing they never read tts lol

Tristan: Yeah, good thing.

Okay, remind me to give you an extra hug for that when we meet.

Dorian: lol

seeing as I probably won't let you go I don't know if an extra hug is even possible

Tristan: Okay, shut up.

And stop trying to make me blush.

Let's just watch the movie.

Tristan: Man, I forgot how good that movie was.

Dorian: lol same

hey tris

Tristan: Yeah?

Dorian: not to make you more anxious or anything

but we have some stuff we have to figure out before we go to bed

Tristan: Oh yeah?

Dorian: so we're meeting at moondoe at four right?

Tristan: Yup.

Dorian: how will we recognize each other?

Tristan: Oh, that's a good point.

I guess I could wear my TTS scarf?

It's pretty recognizable and I don't think anyone else would be wearing one.

And if they are, you can go and date them.

Dorian: lol

that sounds like a plan

ok tristan I'll see you tomorrow

but for real this time

Tristan: Yeah, see you tomorrow.

Goodnight.

Dorian: night

22 It Can't Be

Monday, October 1, 3:44 PM

Alex sat in the back corner of the Moondoe. His leg
was shaking and the coffee he was holding vibrated in
his hands. He put his cup down and brought his hands
to his lap, where he began fiddling with his scarf. He
reminded himself to take deep breaths — in through
the nose and out through the mouth — and tried to
steady his racing heart.

Alex bit his nails and focused on the swirling bits

of cinnamon floating around in his coffee. He noticed a shadow pass over his table.

"Hey . . ."

Alex's eyes shot up, his heart about to burst from his chest. Then he realized who had spoken to him. Grey eyes creased joyfully, a coy grin spreading across thin lips. Jake Greenspan stood in front of Alex. He ran a hand casually through his hair.

"Oh, hey, Jake," Alex responded, smiling at his classmate. He was a little relieved that it was just his English partner. It was still fifteen minutes away from his meeting time with Dorian, and he wasn't quite ready for their encounter.

"What'ya doin'?" Jake asked. He pulled out the chair in front of Alex and sat in it, not even bothering to ask for permission.

Alex rolled his eyes and grinned. "Oh, just waiting for a friend."

"I can help you find them," Jake offered, his face lighting up. "What do they look like?"

Alex watched Jake's eyes as they scanned the

room. He couldn't suppress a chuckle at how silly Jake looked.

"Honestly?" Alex tucked a loose strand of hair behind his ear. "I don't actually know."

"So . . ." Jake cocked an eyebrow and the corner of his mouth twisted in a smirk. "You're waiting for someone and you don't even know what they look like?"

Alex gave a nervous chuckle and nodded his head in agreement. "Pretty much, yeah. I know, it's kinda weird."

"Eh . . ." Jake shrugged, picking at the black nail polish on his fingers. "I've seen weirder."

Alex couldn't hold back his laugh this time. Watching Jake relax in front of him helped put Alex's mind at ease.

"So . . ." Jake looked back up at Alex. Their eyes met, the blue-grey of Jake's irises shining with something that Alex couldn't quite place. "If you don't know what they look like, how do you know *I'm* not the person you're waiting for?"

Alex smirked and rolled his eyes again. "I sincerely doubt that." He secretly admired Jake for his brashness. "What are the chances of that *actually* happening?"

"I dunno, Tristan. They seem pretty high to me."

Alex froze.

It felt like he was hit by a truck. His stomach dropped and his heart sped up. Everything in his body suddenly tensed.

It couldn't be.

It couldn't be.

There was no way that Jake and Dorian were the same person. If they were . . . If Dorian was Jake . . .

Without realizing what he was doing, Alex stood up. He bolted for the door, leaving his coffee and Jake behind at the table. He pushed past crowds of people. He needed to get out. He needed to escape. He needed fresh air.

"Tristan? Tristan!"

Alex hardly heard the voice behind him calling his nickname. All he could think of was Jake's face looking at him, the sly grin. The *knowing* grin. The grin of somebody who had already figured it out and was waiting for his grand reveal.

"Alex, *wait*! Hang on!"

Alex spun around when he felt Jake's fingers graze his wrist. He was outside, in front of dozens of people, but he didn't care. Nobody else was important. The only thing on his mind was Jake. *Dorian.*

"You *knew!!*" Alex hollered. His fists clenched, nails digging painfully into his palms.

Alex watched as Jake's face suddenly faltered, his expression changing to reveal a sense of dread and unease. "Alex, please! You're shouting, there are people arou —"

"You knew this whole *damn* time, *didn't you*?!"

Jake's eyes darted around as he tried to find his words. Alex could practically see him stumbling around in his own head. "No, Alex! Not this whole time, I pro —"

"When did you find out?"

"Tristan," Jake pleaded. He tried to take a step towards Alex, who immediately backed away. "Aren't you happy to see me?"

"When did you find *out*, Jacob?!" Alex's tone was sharp and venomous. Everything about Jake disgusted him at that moment. *He knew.*

Of course he knew. Dorian always figured things out. He figured everything out.

"I . . ." Jake's voice dropped and his eyes fell. There was something so sad about his expression, Alex almost felt bad for yelling. *Almost.* "I figured it out when we met for coffee. To work on the project."

All week.

"You've known for *that long*, and you never said anything?!"

People were staring. Alex could feel their eyes on him, but he didn't care. He didn't care about anything except Jake. Lying, manipulative Jake, who hid the truth from him for a whole week.

"I didn't want you to be uncomfortable! I wanted to make sure we met on your terms!" Jake looked like he was on the verge of tears, but Alex ignored it. No amount of begging or reasoning would change what Jake had done.

"You watched me fall for you ... *twice*!" Alex knew this wasn't the kind of discussion to have in public. But he didn't care. He didn't care that people were watching and judging. He just stood there, trying to wrap his head around everything that was racing through his mind. "You watched as I had a crush on you in real life and you just ...What ...Let me *squirm*?! Let me be uncomfortable, thinking I was falling for another guy?!"

"It wasn't like that, Tris!"

"What was it like then, Jake?" Alex was shouting, unable to control his anger, to keep his frustration inside. He couldn't believe that his Dorian would do that to him. "When I told you I had a crush on someone in real life and you thought I would leave you, what was *that*? Were you just pretending to be mad?! Pretending you didn't know that it was *you* I was falling for?!"

"I didn't know for sure!"

"*Bullshit*! You knew! And you let me dwell on it! You let me panic! You knew it was eating me up inside and you said *nothing*!"

"Alex, please! I didn't mean to make you feel that

way! That wasn't what I wanted!"

"*Screw* what you wanted! And *screw you*!"

Alex spun around and stormed off. He shoved himself through the crowd of people that had gathered around them. He could hear Jake calling for him, but he ignored it. He couldn't deal with Jake. He couldn't deal with anyone. He couldn't believe that Jake *knew*.

23 *Betrayed*

Monday, October 1, 5:31 PM

Tristan: Very cute, Daisy, using the screen name Flora. Did you know?

Flora: Well, hello to you too!

Tristan: Don't play dumb with me, Daisy. DID YOU KNOW?

Flora: . . .

No, I didn't know. Not until he came back this afternoon. He just told Arjun and me.

Tristan: Swear it.

Flora: Alex . . .

Tristan: SWEAR IT, DAISY. Promise me you didn't know!

Flora: I promise, Alex!

Why is this such a big deal? Aren't you happy that you got to meet him in real life?

Tristan: He LIED to me, Daisy!

He KNEW.

He knew the whole time and he didn't tell me! He just sat there! With that information! He kept it from me!

Flora: That's not that bad, though. So he didn't tell you?

Tristan: You don't get it. I was . . .

I was falling for Jake.

Flora: Oh . . .

Tristan: YEAH.

He knew I was falling for him! He knew that I was struggling with those feelings and that I felt guilty. And I felt AWFUL because I thought I was, like, emotionally cheating on him or something! And he let it happen.

Flora: Yeah, that's not good.

Tristan: I told Dorian that I had a crush on Jake.

Flora: Oh.

Tristan: Yeah.

Flora: What did he say?

Tristan: He spouted some bullshit about how crushes are fine so long as I don't act on them.

I CANNOT believe it! I TOLD HIM and he just sat there! He knew the truth and he didn't admit it and he let me stress about it!

It was tearing me UP inside, Daisy! I felt horrible! Why would he do that?!

Flora: Alex, I'm sure he didn't mean to make you upset.

Tristan: He. Knew.

Flora: I know, I know. And that's awful. He should have told you. What he did was wrong.

But I know Jake. And he adores you. And he feels so bad about it. He's in his room right now, with Arjun trying to talk to him.

Tristan: I don't give a DAMN what he's doing right now.

Flora: Alex!

This really isn't like you!

Tristan: Are you on his side or my side, Daisy?

Flora: There are no sides, Alex. There are two people who are hurt, who really care about each other, who want to reconcile.

Tristan: No. There's a dick who lied to the person he claimed to "love" and there's someone who was hurt by said dick.

I don't want to reconcile.

I don't want to "work this out."

I don't want to see him again.

He's an asshole.

And he obviously doesn't respect me.

Flora: Alex . . .

Tristan: Daisy, I'm done. I'm done with him. I'm done with this. I'm done talking about it. I've made up my mind.

Flora: Okay . . .

You should probably let him know that. He seems to think there's still a chance for you two.

Tristan: He can shove it up his ass.

Flora: Alex . . .

Tristan: I'm logging off now, Daisy.

Bye.

Flora: Goodbye, Alex.

8:34 PM

Dorian: alex

talk to me

tristan please

don't do this again

don't just cut me out and ignore me!

Tristan: Screw you.

Dorian: okay

that's better than ignoring me

but not by much

look I'm sorry

I never meant for any of this to happen

I never wanted you to get hurt

I just didn't think you'd be ready to meet any time soon

so I didn't want to stress you out

Tristan: And when I said I had a crush on you?!

Dorian: how was I supposed to know that was me?

Tristan: Don't play dumb with me, Jake! You're not that much of an idiot.

Dorian: I didn't want you to freak out tris!

I honestly thought if I told you you'd get all anxious and stuff

Tristan: And when you accused me of falling for someone else?!

Knowing PERFECTLY WELL that it was YOU?!

Dorian: I didn't know for sure!

Tristan: STOP IT. Stop LYING to me, Dorian!

Dorian: I'm not lying! I was scared!

I love you tris

I loved you then and I love you right now

I was afraid of losing you!

you think I'm not just as terrified of all of this?

this is all new to me too tristan

and I made a mistake!

don't pretend like you've never made a mistake

maybe freaked out a bit and done something stupid and selfish

because I sure as hell know you've done that!

you're right. I shouldn't have thought you liked anyone else

and you're right. when I found out it was me that you had a crush on I probably should have told you the truth

but I didn't

and I'm sorry

tristan?

please talk to me

don't do this again

please

dammit!

there's only so much of this that I can take tris

please talk to me alex

24

Cold Shoulder

Tuesday, October 2, 6:09 PM

Dorian: tristan

just talk to me

you promised me you would communicate with me

you said you wouldn't do this again

let's just talk it out

can we meet?

please?

8:49 PM

Jacob

talk 2 me pls

dont ignore me

tristan this is killing me

Alex

I didn't answer your IMs, what makes you think I want you to text me?

Jacob

alex pls just meet with me

so we can talk

Alex

Not interested, Jacob.

Go away please.

And don't text me again.

Jacob

just meet with me after class tmrrw

i promis 2 keep it short and after that u dont ever have 2 see me again

tristan pls

Wednesday, October 3, 5:13 PM

Dorian: you weren't in class

you're ignoring my texts

I don't know what to do tris

I'm so completely lost right now

just tell me how to fix this

I miss you

please

I said I was sorry!

I told you how bad I felt and how much I wish I had acted differently

but there's nothing I can do to change any of that

can you please just talk to me?

I still love you tris

ok

I give up

not on us

never on us

but on this

you obviously don't want to answer me

so I'll be here

if or when you are ever ready to talk

I just hope it's soon

cause I'm heartbroken

so . . .

bye for now tris

Monday, October 8, 5:42 PM

Dorian: hey tristan

it's been a week since we talked last

just . . .

wanted to let you know that I missed you

Tuesday, October 9, 6:33 PM

"Alejandro Diego Marquez!"

"What do you want, Daisy?"

"I swear to god, if you don't talk to Jake, I am coming straight over there and kicking some god damn sense into you!"

"Go away, Daisy."

"For the love of . . . Alex, I don't think I can take another night of his damn crying! It's like having a puppy!"

"He's crying?"

"You dumped him. Of course he's crying!"

"I didn't . . . I didn't DUMP him exactly . . ."

"Oh, my apologies. You ignored him for over a week after screaming at him in public? You two still boyfriends after that? Because I'm pretty damn sure Jake thinks you dumped him!"

"I just needed some time . . . to process stuff."

"Time's up, Alex! If you want to break up with him, DO IT. If not, TALK TO HIM. But don't leave the poor man in limbo. You're better than that."

"I can't . . . He knew, Daisy."

"Yeah, yeah, he knew. You know how many times you've said that to me? 'He knew, Daisy! He knew!' So WHAT?! You know what else he knew? He knew that you were shy and if he had introduced himself before you were ready to meet, you would have pulled away! Oh, wait a minute, that's LITERALLY WHAT HAPPENED ANYWAY!"

"He's just saying that."

"No, he's not! Because that's what I WOULD DO. I wouldn't have told you if I was in Jake's position!"

"But . . ."

"BUT WHAT, ALEJANDRO?!"

"But when I told him about the crush?"

"He made a mistake! Don't forgive him for that! I don't care! Just don't leave him waiting, hoping that you'll take him back."

Silence. . . .

"So what's it going to be, Alex?"

"I can't just go back and talk to him and pretend nothing's changed."

"Why not?"

"Because everything is different . . ."

"What exactly is different?"

"Well, I mean . . . for one thing, he's Jake."

"Yes. Dorian, the guy you had a crush on, is Jake, the other guy you had a crush on. So?"

"And we met."

"You had already met Jake. What's new?"

"And I yelled at him. In public."

"You act like you've never yelled at anyone before. Alex, you've got the shortest temper I've ever seen. It's damn frustrating sometimes but I love you anyway."

"And I told him not to talk to me."

"I can assure you, if you talked to him, he'd answer. Unlike somebody else I know . . ."

"I can't do this, Daisy."

"Too bad. You have to. Because otherwise, I'm going over to your place, kidnapping you and bringing you straight here."

"Daisy . . ."

"You think I'm joking. I can assure you, I am not. Look, Alex, do you still love him?"

"That is such a loaded question."

"Don't think about it. Just answer. Do you still have feelings for Dorian?"

"Yeah . . ."

"Good. Then talk to him. You don't have to get back together with him. Just listen to him, hear his side PROPERLY and then make your decision after that. Got it?"

"Yeah."

"If I don't hear Jake screaming that you answered him by tomorrow morning, I'm marching over there. Got it?"

"Yes! Geeze, Daisy!"

"Good. I love you, Alex. You're an idiot, but I love you."

"I really hate you sometimes. But I love you too."

"Goodnight, Alex."

"'Night, Daisy."

25 *First Date Redo*

Tuesday, October 9, 8:38 PM

Tristan: Hey.

Dorian: holy shit

hi

I'm really trying my best to seem calm right now but for the record I'm completely freaking out

Tristan: Noted.

So Dorian . . .

There's this guy at school.

And I was friends with him.

Good friends.

And I think I messed things up. And I could use some advice.

Dorian: . . .

??

ok I'll bite

tell me about this friend

Tristan: He's really important to me. More important than I can express in words. He means so much to me . . .

But recently I found out he was keeping a big secret from me. And, well, I got mad at him. And we haven't spoken since.

Dorian: ok

this friend of yours

did he mean to hurt you by keeping this secret?

Tristan: I don't think he did . . . not anymore. But I thought so at the time.

Dorian: you know tris

people keep secrets for lots of reasons

sometimes they hide the truth because they're worried that it might hurt someone they care about

did you ever ask him why he kept it a secret?

Tristan: No, but I should have.

My friend Rose, she said that he was probably hiding the truth from me because he wanted me to learn it on my own terms, at my own pace.

Dorian: rose seems pretty wise

Tristan: She can be.

Dorian: so now that you know that your friend never intended to hurt you . . .

where are things going to go from there?

Tristan: I don't know yet. I figured I could talk to him. I haven't spoken to him in a while.

Not since it happened.

Dorian: how long ago was that?

Tristan: More than a week.

Dorian: that's a long time to go without talking to someone you care about

Tristan: I know.

And I feel awful about it.

I really want to tell him I'm sorry, but I don't know how.

Dorian: well you can always practise on me

Tristan: Okay . . .

I'm sorry that I got so angry at you. I now know that your intentions weren't bad. I wish I could have seen it at the time.

I'm also sorry that I yelled at you in public. Definitely not one of my finer moments.

And mostly, I'm sorry for leaving you hanging, not knowing whether we could go back to the way things were between us. Not knowing if we were even together anymore.

As friends. Of course.

Dorian: of course

Tristan: And I'm sorry that I didn't come to my senses earlier.

Dorian: you know what?

Tristan: What?

Dorian: I think if you said that to your friend he'd forgive you

Tristan: You really think so?

Dorian: I do

I mean . . .

if I were in his position I'd forgive you

Tristan: Thanks, Dor.

Dorian: hey tris

Tristan: Yeah?

Dorian: I've also been struggling with some stuff at school can I talk it out with you?

Tristan: Of course.

Dorian: so there's this guy

he's . . .

well he's everything to me

and recently I made him upset by doing something stupid

and I apologized to him

a lot

more than I've ever apologized before

but he didn't forgive me

instead he ignored me

for a while

and it really hurt

I was sad for a long time

it wasn't the first time he's ignored me like that

and it took a lot out of me

Tristan: Have you spoken to him about this yet?

Dorian: not yet

he's going through his own stuff right now and I feel awful
bringing it up

but part of me feels like I need to tell him

otherwise we'll never be able to move on

Tristan: Yeah, I get that.

Dorian: and I honestly can't imagine my life without him

I really can't

and I'd take him back in a heartbeat if he'd have me

but . . .

but there's a part of my mind that wonders what if it happens again?

I honestly don't know if I could handle that

Tristan: I think you should tell him.

I have a feeling that this friend of yours doesn't know just how much he's hurt you.

If you tell him the truth about how you're feeling, I think it might help him realize just how hard you're taking it.

I have a question, Dor . . .

Dorian: ya?

Tristan: If he apologized, would you forgive him?

Dorian: without a doubt

but I don't need an apology

I know he didn't mean it

and I know he's sorry

I just . . . I want to make sure that nothing like that happens again

Tristan: Trust me, if you explain that to him, I'd be willing to bet that he'd promise never to ignore you again. He'd promise to never leave you hanging and to talk things out, even if it's hard for him.

Dorian: if he made a promise like that it would help so much

that would mean the world to me

Tristan: I think you two might even end up being stronger for it. Because once you communicate properly with someone, dealing with problems gets a little easier.

Dorian: I agree

I wish I could give you a big hug right now

Tristan: I mean, this virtual hug is nice.

But . . .

Didn't you say the other day that we live close to each other?

Dorian: I did.

Tristan: Would you want to meet up at some point? You could give me that hug for real.

And we could finally see each other for the first time.

Dorian: ya

that would be nice

I'd like that

you know

tomorrow's a school day

want to maybe grab some coffee after?

we can just talk

Tristan: I'd like that, Dorian.

Dorian: perfect

I'll see you after school

Tristan: So . . .

Not to spoil the mood or anything, but I'm kind of a few episodes

behind on Basker.

Dorian: it's still early

wanna watch one of those basker episodes now?

Tristan: There is literally nothing that I would rather do right now.

Dorian: excellent

lemme just grab a torrent

Tristan: Yeah, I need to download it too.

Dorian: I've missed this tris

Tristan: Yeah, me too.

Dorian: oh

um . . .

apparently daisy says hi

and she says she's happy she doesn't have to beat you up

Tristan: Tell her to stuff it.

Dorian: yeah no thanks

I'm not telling aj's girlfriend to stuff it

lol

oh that was fast

my episode is done downloading

Tristan: Mine just finished, too. Ready?

Dorian: play

Tristan: That was a good episode. It's nice that the boys got to meet each other after so long.

Dorian: ya

Tristan: Okay, I've gotta get up early tomorrow. I should head to bed.

Dorian: same

goodnight tris

Tristan: Goodnight, Dorian.

I love you.

Dorian: I love you too

Acknowledgements

This book would not have been possible without the love and support of my friends and family, both irl and online, old and new.

A special thank you to Purple, my encyclopedia; Max, my real life Dorian; and the AGA server, my support system. You made me feel like I had a story worth telling, and actively encouraged me to share it with the world.

Thank you to my editor, Kat Mototsune, who looked at a manuscript and saw potential, despite the word count!

Thank you to Elizabeth and Allanah, for being willing to beta my work when it was nearly twice as long as it is now! And thanks to Andre, Xander and Aurora for being my cheering squad!

Most importantly, thank *you*, the reader, who picked up this book and wanted to see where it would take you. I hope you enjoyed reading about Tristan and Dorian and that you carry their journeys with you. It's readers like you who inspire me to continue writing!

MARQUIS

Québec, Canada